Where the Best Began

Stories of a Boy on the American Prairie

By L. D. Bergsgaard

First published by Dog Ear Publishing
4010 W. 86th Street, Ste H
Indianapolis, IN 46268
www.dogearpublishing.net

ISBN: 978-1-4575-1034-2

This book is printed on acid-free paper.

This book is a work of fiction. Places, events, and situations in this book are purely fictional and any resemblance to actual persons, living or dead, is coincidental.

Printed in the United States of America

Cover photograph © copyrighted by James Lindquist. All rights reserved.

Dedication

Dedicated to our mother, Genevieve Cecelia Lang Bergsgaard, creator of Farmer John and other fantastical characters of wonder and joy; to our father, Clarence, for his wisdom, patience and tolerance; to my brother, Mike Bergsgaard, for his expert guidance and intellectual inspiration, the teachers and librarians who taught me to read and gave me the life-long love of books, and the friends of my youth who still live in my heart.

Acknowledgments

Without Donna's encouragement, suggestions, and expert editing abilities, this work would not have been completed. I thank my wife of forty years for her devotion and loyalty.

I'm indebted to Jim Lindquist for the photograph used on the book's cover and to the wonderful boy, Adler Siebenaler who struck a pose that was remarkably similar to the stories' hero, Moose.

I'm eternally grateful for Ruby, my faithful steed, upon whose back I write with ease.

And to my daughters, Anne and Kate, who keep me forever young.

Introduction

It's true, what many say. Time and age have a way of rounding off the edges and making jagged pieces of the past seem clear and smooth and bright. But for those of us growing up in the small prairie town of Mandan, North Dakota, in the 1950s, those truly were times when every day was an adventure, every neighbor was a story, and everyone belonged somewhere because we were all connected and trusted others to know that. Since those days I have travelled, I have seen parts of the world that I would not have dared to imagine I'd visit when I was young. I have met many interesting people and have known the challenges of life; across that span of time, across the globe and throughout my years, there has been one thing that is a constant for me and that is the memory of the lessons, the friends and the opportunities I enjoyed in that cultural, historical, and geographical nexus of our great country. Whatever measure I take of times, places and people today, it is in comparison to the gold standard of my childhood in the West. That was where the best began for me, for my family and for my friends and these are our stories.

Only with age do we have the ability to comprehend how differently we look at our world when we are ten compared to when we've arrived at what sociologists have termed middle age or what we, as kids, called old farts. At ten, we can't know how fast time flies, how days just begin and then they're over. At ten, the clock most often stood still, especially in the classroom or at your cousin's dance recital. At sixty, we celebrate the 4th of July and then scramble to purchase Christmas presents. As a boy, the time between Thanksgiving and Christmas could be measured with an hour glass seemingly tipped on its side and not days. I wrote this collection of short stories from a ten-year-old boy's eyes with the interpretation of the mind and recollection of a sixty-year-old man.

The characters in this collection of short stories are all a product of my imagination. The events and places are all, well if not real, at least live in my memories. The independent short stories are arranged from the calendar of a boy exploring life in a small town which touts itself as "Where the West Begins." And so, I take the kaleidoscope of time in my hands, now scarred by life and covered with age spots, give it a gingerly twist, and I'm back where my heart will always be.

BUTTERFLIES

"She looks like Old Lady Greely's goat—even got the beard and yellow eyes." Melonhead offered his description of the teacher I'd be seeing for the first time in less than an hour. Today was the beginning of another school year, actually the beginning of the entire year for kids. For the adults the calendar changed on January 1st, for us, it was the first day of school.

"You don't know that." I made the bold assertion then ducked Melonhead's round-house. Melonhead was a burly boy with a stout body that supported the source of his nickname, but he was getting entirely too predictable with his responses, an observation Mickey had made the previous week when I had slipped quickly away from the headlock Melon would have clamped on me had I not expected it.

"I seen her this summer, in June when we was in Medora." He had the hide of a rhinoceros and was persistent in furthering his assertions, many which were notably false. On the other hand, he had been in Medora. I knew that because I tended to his calico cat, Mel, while his family was on vacation. And my mother had mentioned that Miss Martin was moving from the cattle country 'out West.' That was the problem assessing the accuracy of any of Melonhead's stories. There was always a taste of the truth he rolled up in his bologna sandwiches.

"We was walking past the school and out she flies, down the boardwalk. She's so mean and ugly, the dogs ran and hid under the wagons and they was mean and ugly dogs." His arms flew as he expanded the exposition that had the potential to instill such fear in me that I would crawl back home and lock myself in the upstairs closet until my parents promised to move across the river to Bismarck where there would be a new school and no Miss Martin. For that matter, perhaps I could transfer to the Reform School. After all, the Old Man had promised the Reformatory, just down the road a piece, would always have a room for me. I wondered if there was a small room, with a cot and bars on the windows, which had a name plate reading 'Larry' or maybe 'Moose' outside the grey steel door.

"…and then they had tied their horses to the hitching post in front of the saloon and when she walked past, the horses reared back and pulled the post out of the ground. My cousin says one died of fright and the other three are still running upright on two hind legs."

The first day of school was full of excitement and apprehension. Full of fears but not the kind you get on the back of a rank cayuse. It was more the fear of the unknown and the fear of the inability to point your steed towards your own destiny, down your chosen dusty trail. And at least according to Melonhead, I was headed for a wreck.

I fell behind Mike, Willie, Sherry, and Melonhead. Mickey and I shuffled along, he in his Keds and me in the cowboy boots that three days ago, I had been so proud of. Brown and white with stitching of horses etched on the tops. Today they felt wooden. The heel of the boot would hit the ground long before the toe would catch up and strike with a slap. I felt clumsy and conspicuous – a boy with the kind of reckless bravado Miss Martin would surely seek to temper. Three days ago, my mother took my brother, Mike, and me shopping at F. W. Woolworth's. Mike had strayed off in search of a multi-zippered, black-leather jacket he would never be allowed to own. Being the youngest, I had to have my mother's guidance in wardrobe matters. She made a bee line past the slims, the regulars, straight to the husky jeans. She held them up – they would have been large enough for Uncle Herman to keep a pig in his pants.   The annual shopping spree was the onset of my personal struggle of the New Year. In the first grade, it didn't matter. I could have worn the sheet off my bed and a pillow case for a hat and no one would have cared. But now it was important to be cool—not dashing, but at least cool. Hard to even fake cool in your huskies, especially with the billboard size brand tag on the back announcing 'HUSKY' to any kid who hadn't noticed.

So here I was clomping and clapping down the cracked and heaved side-walk wearing my husky jeans and a plaid shirt with metal buttons and the short sleeves rolled up. A couple of dozen paces ahead was Mike, with his two-tone bowling shirt, slim jeans rolled at the cuffs, loafers with shiny pennies on the top, and the beginning of a duck-tail, a fashion I had no use for since it seemed to hold the potential for yet another nickname or proclaim me to be the hoodlum I had no desire of becoming.

The janitor, Mr. Bernard whose name had morphed into Barnyard, blocked the school entrance. No one entered until the appointed time of 8:45. Children could have been minutes from freezing to death or inches from being snatched by a twister, but if it was 8:44, there was no access to the salvation on the other side of those doors. Mr. Barnyard, who was often called Senior, to distinguish him from his son who was also a custodian, knew it was time when the bell rang. He begrudgingly opened the door, as if it pained his soul to allow the careless urchins on the waxed floors he'd spent the summer polishing to a gleam with his new electric buffer. He couldn't have been more inhospitable than if Ringling Brothers had backed up the entire circus for unloading in his school. My new boots made hollow hoof-beat sounds that echoed even as Mickey and I made our way up the stairs to the second floor. We were moving up in the world. A couple more years and we'd be on the third floor. Up there as sixth graders—the kings and queens of the castle until the seventh grade when we'd move back down the pyramid into peasantry while the high schoolers would hold dominion…I was beginning to wonder if this was a cycle without an ending before death.

Senior's son, Ronald, waited outside our classroom, barring the door just as he'd seen his father doing so effectively. "No one goes inside until I say so." This was the young janitor's big day. He even had a speaking role. "First you have to get your locker assignments from me." Lockers came with promotion. Until this year, I'd been relegated to the cloak room, a name I never understood. Sherlock Holmes was the last guy on earth to wear a cloak. "Line up, alphabetically, in a straight line and no talking." It was 8:46, and already the 'no talking' rule was being evoked. How can I learn if I can't talk?

Being a B, I jumped in front. It had been my place since the beginning. There were no A's in Mandan. Things occasionally change, sometimes as fast as two students butting in front of me. "You an A?" the blond girl a head taller than me asked. "We're A's. I'm Sally and this is my brother, Billy. We just moved here…" This would change everything. When I ate, went to the bathroom, where I sat, I mean, I'd enjoyed the rank of being a B, of being first, forever. And just that fast, two kids, who looked alike, and whom I couldn't even see over, ejected me from the throne.

Billy and Sally accepted the first two lockers. I moved forward to take number three. My eyes cast to the floor in front of Junior as the young Ronald was called by older kids. His worn boots were caked with red floor-sweeping compound. "Coat, and caps, boots and books. That's it, nothing else. No food, drinks or baby sisters." Junior had a sense of humor –something he must have got from his mother before she ran off with Eddy the mailman and left Senior and Junior to make what they could of life as school custodians.

Billy was taller, tanner, and blonder than Sally. His locker was number two.

"Where you from?" I thought it best to welcome him despite my plight.

"You writing a book?" he spit out faster than a cat with a cough.

"Just ignore him. He's still mad because we had to move here." Sally had a kind face and a friendly spirit. "We moved from Hollywood, California, and Bill played on the team that would be going to the Little League World Series. So now he'll never get to play."

"Not here in this hick town I won't." He'd perfected a scowl and an attitude that could earn him a humbling experience courtesy of one of our hick hoodlums each of whom had their own carefully crafted ducktails, black jackets, and knives. It was rumored that the worst of the bunch were girls and that they had zip guns that fired real .22 bullets. Another possibility that defied imagining.

"What position do you play? Our team needs a couple more players," I said.

Billy ignored my offer. "He's a catcher," Sally politely answered.

A catcher? No, I'm the catcher. Our team doesn't need a catcher. As I was given to performance block, my mind stalled. Is this day a dream? A nightmare? It was bad enough that they had bumped me down to third in line, now Billy was threatening to bump me out to right field. My comfortable world was unraveling.

"Moose, put your stuff in the locker and let's get inside," Mickey whispered.

Mickey's urging set me back in the direction of reality and a punch on the arm by a passing high schooler placed me in the doctor's office.

....

Just yesterday, that arm had been the target of a medical assault usually reserved for the condemned. If somebody had marked on the calendar that Wednesday was the day an atomic bomb would be dropped on Mandan I couldn't have dreaded that day more than the date set for my medical exam. Up to that point I was blissfully ignorant of the fact that, like the shoemaker's shoeless kids, I, the son of a nurse, had not been inoculated against the multitude of exotic diseases that stalked all unprotected children in those days. Whooping Cough, Diphtheria, Lockjaw, the names alone were enough to make a guy pull the bed covers over his head and not come out except maybe for Christmas and his birthday. Apparently feeling a sudden urgency to compensate for my vulnerability, my mother pulled a few strings at the clinic and got me in late in the afternoon—weeks before I was scheduled to go. Dr. Wheeler's office was empty. I was the last patient of the day. I despised the exam, but I liked Dr. Wheeler. He was there when I was born and he was there for every malady I had struggled through since then. He was gentle, wise, and confident – the things you'd want in one of the few humans licensed to slice, saw, and sew other people.

The door to the examination room swung open. An imposing man in a white lab coat looked down his glasses at me. "Okay—come on, you're next." It was Dr. Mueller. The doctor my mother worked for in the surgical room. The doctor she called 'the butcher.' The guy who'd taken off the wrong leg for poor old Mr. Tuttle, the diabetic square dancer and accordion player. It was said that Mr. Tuttle, the pastor's brother, never missed a step. No wonder she was able to get my appointment moved up so easily.

I stood weakly. "I'm supposed to see Dr. Wheeler."

"No, you're supposed to see me and here I am. Now get in here, you're the last of the day." He tugged at my arm and propelled me into the small drab room. It smelled of alcohol and bad deeds. "Up on the table young man."

I sat on the crinkling meatcutter's paper covering the table barely able to hold my water. My butt puckered and my knees shook. The butcher! I eyed his hands for the glint of a scalpel or fresh blood and held my arms close to my torso. I could be the next Mr. Tuttle. He used a customized flashlight to peer into my ears, and nose, and then poked a Popsicle stick in my mouth causing me to gag. As if trying to set a new record for the fastest exam, he pulled out the rubber hammer from his black leather tool kit and gave my kneecap a shot. He missed and it hurt. I knew what was supposed to happen and didn't want another kneecapping so I shot my foot up with an exaggerated reflex. Right up into the man's crotch. He must have had his shorts lined with lead since he only scowled all the more ominously.

"OO-oops, sorry! I wasn't trying to kick you," I cried.

"Stand up and take your pants down, your underwear too." No waiting for revenge to be served cold in this office.

Exposing my privates was something new, and an act for which I had an innate aversion. I wasn't sure whether to wish for my mother to be there or my father. Not wanting to hint that I had something to hide, I complied. Without looking and without hesitation, his bare hand locked on my testicles and he ordered me to cough. I couldn't. I could have cried. I could have gurgled. I could have filled my shorts if they had been on, but I couldn't cough. Moreover, I saw no connection between his holding my testicles and me pretending to cough.

"I said cough, kid, now cough, dammit!" The man was an animal. He had my privates covered with his big furry hand and wanted me to serenade him with a cough. Should I have farted when he looked into my ear? As much as I was tempted to flee, I realized the beast had me locked in tight and I feared making even the slightest movement that would cause him to tighten his grip on the one thing I knew I wanted to keep to myself. I finally forced a huffy cough from deep in my chest; regrettably I also forced my bladder to evacuate. I peed on the man's hand and, to make matters worse, I began laughing involuntarily and uncontrollably. He jerked his hand away as though it had been singed and leaped to the running water at the sink. "Nurse, get in here quick—the kid just drained his tank—good god!" Then he turned to me with a wicked sneer and muttered, "Think that was funny do you? And, nurse, bring the vaccines, the ones in the extra large hypos, you know, the ones we use on the horses."

A nurse dressed in a starched white uniform and sporting a distracting wart on her nose tip, came in with a tray and the giggles left me as quickly as they had appeared. Needles the size of number 10 framing nails lay ready on the stainless steel tray. The doctor made notes and whispered to the aged nurse, probably about my lack of control as the nurse cleaned the floor.

"Turn over on the table face down," he ordered.

Oh, Geez, if he could do those things to my face, what would the fiend do behind my back? I crawled slowly, pulling my jeans up as I flattened on the paper sheet. It sounded like Katten the cat crawling on the Old Man's newspaper as she prepared it for urination.

"Leave your pants down, son," the nurse said and with the swiftness of a sushi chef pushed a thermometer so deep into my rectum that I could taste Vaseline.

"In your butt or your arm, Kid?"

What in my butt? My butt had all it could handle no matter what he had in mind. "My arm…I give up…anything….just don't…." And with that the doctor plunged the needle into my buttocks with the speed and flourish of a pirate in a swordfight. I don't know how the horses he worked on lived through it. And it may have been my imagination, but I'm pretty certain I could actually feel the vaccine pushed into my flesh then radiate slowly from the puncture point.

"This won't hurt," said the nurse just as I began to recover from the assault on my rear. With that, she grabbed the middle finger of my right hand and squeezed until it was purple. Out of nowhere metal flashed and she stabbed the ripened digit with a lancet that stung like a fast fuse firecracker. Then, a long proboscis from her mouth to my finger and the blood began to float toward her pinched lips.

"All right, and now the D.P.T. in your arm and you're done, you little…" That was when I fainted.

. . . .

I eased sideways into my classroom. Miss Martin had been busy preparing for our class—must have had time after she terrorized the hounds and horses of Medora. Autumn leaves adorned the bulletin board between the bathrooms. A penmanship chart wrapped around the top of three walls. The world map hung on another wall. I'd planned many trips on the outdated maps in my previous classrooms. Next to the evidence that the Earth was flat was the 'Helpers' chart. I coveted the hall-monitor position which required at least a ten minute round trip out of the class. Last year, I'd even stretched the outing by five extra minutes. I hurried to the board to check the assignments. 'Hall Monitor: William Adams.' I scanned for my name and found it on the bottom of the board, behind 'Bathroom Monitor.' I would be relegated to the crappers.

On the front chalkboard, in letters the size of a tall gopher was printed, 'Welcome, My name is Miss Martin.' I froze in the back of the room. How could I face an entire year of this?

"Larry, take your desk. It's number three." That voice, it was as Melon had described—enough to stampede a herd of horses and make dogs howl. With shoulders slumped I stumbled to the front to find desk number three. Miss Martin was indeed uglier than a goat, the rear end. She was taller and older than Moses. Her black dress hid her ankles but not the dark shoes that resembled those remnants of the wicked witch under the house. She knitted her eyebrows and frowned in disapproval as I passed under her glare to the safety of my desk. It was obvious why she wore the title, Miss.

I carried the Piggly Wiggly grocery bag packed with my stuff. It was the same 'stuff' I'd emptied from last year's desk. The brown paper bag had lain, happily forgotten, under my bed the entire summer. A few unused pencils, a couple of cat-eye marbles, a box of tissues, and my old eraser. I'd elected to stay with the old gum eraser. She'd been with me for two years, wiping out my mistakes and never passing judgment. Like an old friend she would be by my side. I slipped the paper straw and a week's supply of spitballs under the two notebooks. The ammo had dried like corn over the summer. The notebooks were a bit ragged but still worthy of *my* notations and calculations. Last year, I only used about ten pages and half of those ended in the wastebasket. On the top page there was a rather artful rendering of Cathy P. which I had doodled after she'd tattled on me for decorating her ample posterior with a snowball. But that was back in my carefree youth— now I had bigger problems which stood in the form of a forbidding Miss Martin looking over her charges.

I settled into desk number three. It seemed like a friendly enough place to spend a year of my life. She squeaked a bit when I opened her top. Miss Martin could order Senior to order Junior to oil the hinges if it annoyed her. The desk smelled of cleaning solvents. Not so much as a crumb in the pencil tray. I dumped the contents of the bag in the bottom of the metal desk. That was as neat as it would be for the rest of the year. A barely noticeable MB was carved into the desktop. Could this have been my brother's desk? Or my grandfather's? They bore the same name and I have no doubt each would have thought himself important enough to be remembered for posterity if only by two letters carved into an old desk.

Miss Martin's voice, sounding similar to a nagging raven, droned on as I took a measure of my surroundings. My report cards usually noted a frailty in my deportment. I, it was often alleged, did not pay attention in class and I showed little in the way of initiative. I never bothered to correct the flaws in the teachers' observations and notations. I did pay attention but not necessarily to their priorities. I paid attention to the birds in the trees singing pleasant songs through the open windows. I carefully minded the clock. I doubt if anyone in class was more aware of the number of minutes and seconds to recess or the end of class. I was acutely aware of the first snowfall. I paid close attention to the nurse, my mother, when she gave her annual presentation on hygiene. I was so focused when she brought out dentures suitable for a Tyrannosaurus and a waist high toothbrush that the clock actually slowed even more in its inexorable march toward my graduation still years away. Did the other kids really think we used those things in our house? My focus sharpened into total embarrassment when my mother endeavored to explain that, in using our toothbrush, we should slip it in our mouths with toothpaste— but she didn't say slip, she had a miscue with her own dentures and said "shit"…shit the toothpaste into our mouths—another superhuman feat for the books and another humiliation from which I could never recover. My mother? She laughed and said simply, "Oops, my dentures *slipped*, children..." From behind me, Mickey whispered, "Your mom is a really funny lady—you're lucky to have her." Yeah, most of the time.

....

The one time I did demonstrate initiative, it caused me life-long trauma and ended the steady progress I had been making toward becoming a master painter or maybe a cartoonist for "Gasoline Alley." In the first grade I had worked my craft as an artist using the reliable but limited Crayola box of 7. In truth, I only needed the red, green and blue, but I convinced my mother that this was too limited a palette to work from and that my development would be enhanced if she would provide me with the superior box of 48.

As Thanksgiving of that year drew near, I was offered an opportunity not only to show initiative but to show my artistry when the teacher, Miss Shank, distributed outlines of particularly robust turkeys featuring huge fans of feathers for tails. I had just finished a spectacular Fuchsia feather when I noticed Ms. Shank move in behind my desk at the end of the row….to admire my work, no doubt. I had fashioned the first psychedelic bird, long before anyone could even spell the word. I interrupted my work and leaned back a bit to give her the benefit of a full view of my Technicolor Turkey…there was a pause before the praise flowed forth. It must have taken a while for her to process the product of such inventiveness never before seen in a boy my age. But what flowed forth wasn't praise, just a loud pronouncement along the lines that "This, young man, is the most repulsive looking turkey I have ever beheld." And to stress the point, she slapped me on the back of the head … so much for ingenuity…so much for art…so much for creativity and expression.

....

"Moose, get your notebook out, it's time to write about what we did over summer vacation," Mickey's mystical voice whispered from behind. Mickey always paid attention and never failed to bring me back from the pleasant journeys my mind had a habit of taking. 'Summer Vacation,' was going to be the first task of the New Year, as inevitably as being seated alphabetically. This year, I was ready. This year, I had some stories, and unlike a few earlier theses, this one wouldn't be fiction. With a newly sharpened pencil, I skipped over Cathy P.'s portrait and authored a story that Mark Twain would have regarded as worthy of retelling.

Lost in my musings, however, I'd neglected my clock watching duties and was startled when the recess bell rang. The timing was impeccable, the last period in place on the last sentence, and I dashed out the door to freedom like a colt out of the corral gate. The sounds of the playground were those of a finely tuned orchestra. From the dull monotone thud that was Miss Martin's class to shouts of delight, giggles of joy, and cries of freedom as the boys and girls swung to the clouds and whirled on the merry-go-round. The three Cathy's jumped rope. The girls, ever so helpful, wore dresses intended to assist the new teacher sort them out. Cathy P. wore pink, Cathy R. in red, and Cathy Z. wore black and white, "like a zebra," she proudly announced to Miss Martin.

I joined the boys, Willie, Oscar, and Ron, at the circle drawn in the dust. Marbles, cat eyes, steelys, and aggies flew from their fingers employing a variety of shooting techniques. I watched with Mickey peering quietly over my shoulder—the scent of his chocolate milk breath the only evidence that he was there. Soon, Willie, using a steely the size of a golf ball cleaned up and filled his pockets with marbles. His pants looked like a chipmunk's cheeks stuffed with acorns. Throughout the year, the good fortune would move around like a riverboat poker game, each player enjoying a rich man's pocket at least once. And at the end of the year, there was a better than even chance that most would end up with the marbles they began with.

I wandered to the top of the hill where in a few months we'd be sliding down the snow covered slope. I settled next to Mickey and surveyed the playground chaos and eating the orange I'd brought for Miss Martin. "Everything has changed this year, and not for the better. Every time I think I understand this world, they change it."

"If there was no change, there would be no butterflies," Mickey offered.

"But this year doesn't look good. I mean…"

As often happened when I was on the brink of an epiphany a bell rang, a teacher scolded me, or a dog chased me. This time it was the bell.

Senior, now backed-up by the smirking Junior, guarded the heavy doors, turning away any student who'd rolled in the mud or tried to smuggle in any one of an array of interesting but outlawed creatures captured during the break. Free of either, I cleared the inspection and dashed back to class. I tossed my coat in the bottom of the locker and turned right into Billy's chest. Given his surly nature, I expected a shove, a punch, some smart remark and stepped back, fists to my face.

"Expect the unexpected," Uncle Herman, the aged warrior and sage, had instructed me during my first boxing lesson. He followed that advice with a jab to my gut. That exclamation point to his admonition stayed with me far longer than the belly ache it produced.

"Moose, I didn't mean to be such a jerk. I'm really a pitcher. They made me catch just because they wanted the coach's son to pitch. Willie was telling me at recess that your team could use a pitcher."

"We can, Bill, my brother's the pitcher, but he's moving up a league. You and I can practice, bring your glove tomorrow. I'll catch for you."

"Let's get to class. I can hardly wait to see what Miss Martin looks like."

Mickey was right about change. And Billy must have spent more time daydreaming than me if he wanted to get more of Miss Martin's looks. What'd he think that some witch's spell had been broken and she'd transformed into a sweet princess over recess?

I was the last to my seat. Miss Martin tossed me a stern look.

"And now class, I want you to meet Miss Martin." I heard that much and then my eyes met those of the most beautiful woman whoever graced a classroom. Two Miss Martins? Was Alfred Hitchcock directing this debacle?

The Miss Martin with the long black hair and wide brown eyes like a deer fawn stepped forward. "Class, I'm Miss Martin, and I'll be your teacher this year. I'm sorry I couldn't be here for the start of class. I took the train to Medora this weekend and drove on the way back. We had a long detour around a bridge that washed out. I want to thank Miss Rudolph for filling in until I could get here." I was in love and even with my rudimentary math skills could calculate, that if she could just hold on for a few more years, Miss Martin and I would have a beautiful wedding and a wonderful life together.

As usual, Mickey was right, without change there'd be no butterflies.

PUMPKIN DAZE

"Melonhead, you'd better get out here fast, Irma's naked," I whispered loudly just below the level of adult detection. My neck bent back, I waited for the red-haired boy to poke his freckled face out the screenless window to his second floor bedroom. The nervous movement of a crow was evident in the darkness over the gabled roof but no Melonhead. Suddenly, with a grace that threw the black bird into a panic he burst out the wooden door to the balcony, pulling his worn and patched jeans around his waist. Shoeless and taking two, no three steps at a time, he brought his 200 plus pounds to bear on each creaking step.

"Where's she?" he panted. He grabbed my arm and shook me roughly. "Moose, where is she, you little dork?"

"You'll see. Come on, quick...this can't last forever." I set out at a sprint then slowed for my barefoot neighbor trying his best to keep up on the gravel alleyway.

"Slow down," he ordered as only Melonhead could. He caught me and forced the point by twisting the neck of my sweatshirt in a ball and hanging on. My only concern was missing the show, but towing him was like dragging Mr. Johnson's Chrysler Imperial up Snake Hill.

We neared the brown stucco cottage with the moss covered roof and I slowed to a walk not wanting to disturb the scene which had unfolded before our very eyes just moments ago. I led my breathless companion to the base of an apple tree that towered over the cottage roof. The apples had weeks ago been surrendered to our larcenous hands and eager mouths. The ones the birds and bugs had beaten us to crunched under my feet. I looked up and was pleased to see Mickey and Willie were still holding their separate positions. They didn't notice our arrival and were whispering to each other. Willie was pointing. A good sign.

"Mickey is she still..." I asked.

"Shhh." He put a finger to lips that still had the grape Popsicle mustache. We'd each been sharing the frozen treat while casually observing Irma's unoccupied bedroom when she made her debut appearance fresh from the bathtub and into the unmade bed. Stunned would not be doing justice to describe the emotions we felt. Betrayed, perhaps, at how she'd robbed us of our innocence and naivety. Mickey nodded with his monkey-cute face and Mona Lisa smile then waved us up.

Melonhead pushed me aside and hugged the apple tree like a tubby bear cub struggling to reach the lowest branch. "Lift me up, hurry." I wrapped my arms around as much of his soft waist as best I could and pushed up with all my might. A fart squeezed out of one of us, but it didn't gain Melonhead an advantage in his efforts. "Get on the ground." He commanded like the drill sergeant he would later become. I complied like a raw recruit and hit the dirt. No sooner had my hands dug into the fallen autumn leaves when he'd planted his toes into my spine. With the aid of my pals in the trees pulling and grunting, Melonhead reached the catbird's seat. He zeroed in on the reclining, snoring, and nude Irma.

"Shitttt…"was all he could spit out. He reached into his pants pocket and pulled out a fistful of sunflower seeds. They went into his mouth as a bunch and after some strategic maneuvering in his puffed cheeks began flying out with the steadiness and speed of bullets from a machine gun. A master of mastication, he practiced his craft while swinging a bat, applying a head-lock, or saying his bedtime prayers for all I knew.

I reached a spot on a friendly branch behind my big headed friend and had to agree with his assessment. Disappointing, that's what it was. We'd all talked about such matters and a few even fancied ourselves young experts on the female anatomy but not because any of us had ever seen a real live species and this particular exhibition had thrown us a curveball maybe even a knuckleball.

"Whaz ze hell you boys doin' up dere?" The baritone voice with a French accent convinced me we were dealing with Irma's boyfriend or husband, whatever their marital status. "You leetle bastards get down from my tree before I catch you and serve your pri….va…tes to zee cats." He had an ominous way of saying privates…stretching it out as though he'd already verbally grabbed them.

He was still outside the fence and in the alley, so I estimated we, or at least I, could likely escape without feeding the three mangy felines that slinked unfettered in all parts of the neighborhood. I swung down from my perch using the lowest branch. I landed on my feet, took two steps then was staggered as Melonhead broke his long jump by using my backside as a landing pad. I heard something snap in my back but had my private parts to protect so I sprung forward spitting dead leaves from my bleeding mouth and headed for the hills, literally.

Behind me, I could hear that witless Frenchman laughing as though he'd just put the run on the *Bouche* from the Louvre. I'd heard the Old Man tell Mom that Frenchie had been in the Resistance and was a killer. He'd met Irma, I'd overheard, in a blackout in England during the war, but at the time I wasn't certain how all of that fit together.

I passed Melonhead, no great feat, especially uphill, but at least now Frenchie could catch the biggest prize first and I was happy to allow Melon that honor. More for the cats, I speculated. Willie and Mickey were waiting at Snake Hill, in the cave when I arrived. Actually I fell into the dugout we fancied as our hideout, a refuge that no adult knew about or would bother to climb into. Adults didn't get off sidewalks and were smart enough not to traipse over a hill named for the rattlesnakes who resided thereabouts.

Willie had the candle lit and was pulling the second to last Winston from the pack he'd pilfered two days ago from his mother, when Melonhead charged in and dove to the rear of our little retreat. He panted like a bulldog in the Sahara and while he tried to speak, he couldn't. Only guttural sounds, a little like the ones made by the real Mummy—the Boris Karloff Mummy –escaped his purple lips. Willie lit the bent smoke, coughed twice then smiled as we passed around the odious rite of passage without speaking.

"That was awful," Willie finally offered in succinct summary.

"We'd have been crucified," Mickey added with awe and wonder.

"I mean Irma, that's not what I expected…she was so large and…" …and hairy…very hairy…much harrier than all of our dads combined, I concluded in my mind. "That's not what women are supposed to look like," Willie finished then took the smoke as though a puff on the forbidden weed would eradicate the haunting picture from his mind forever.

"You guys are full of crap. You don't know what you're talking about. Ain't none of you seen nothing before?" Melonhead had caught his breath enough to belittle us and perhaps buy some time before continuing his account of what we had collectively witnessed. Being the oldest and the largest carried some weight in our neighborhood, but it didn't count for much when it came to quick thinking.

"How'd you become the know it all? Peeking through the keyhole at your sister?" Willie asked. The question was answered with a well aimed fist to Willie's shoulder knocking him into the candle and putting us in the dark but for the dying embers of the cigarette. I fumbled for the matches and lit the candle. Willie still lay on the dirt floor moaning. Melonhead could pack a punch like Joe Louis, even from a seated position.

"Anyone else want some?" Melonhead asked, a crooked smile widening with his restored dignity. "I seen pictures of a bunch of naked women. And they don't look nothing like ole Irma. They..."

"Where'd you see them," I bravely challenged knowing that not even Melonhead could throw a punch the length of two bodies and he was too lazy to actually move.

The candlelight danced on his pumpkin like grin. The grin still haunts me fifty years later. "Old Bicycle Bill, that's where, dinkus. He had 'em in his bike shop."

"My Uncle Billy? Aunt Tillie won't allow no such pictures. You're lying. They're Presbyterians you know," I added to cement my argument. Our Aunt Tillie wouldn't even allow her poor brother to smoke in his own room or drink anywhere on the property she owned and he tended. I'd heard our father say Tillie ran Bill into the ground and agreed that he most certainly looked like he'd spent time underfoot. Because he was deaf and never spoke much to kids, it was hard to convey my sympathy for his plight, but being the youngest, I thought Uncle Bill and I knew something about being trod upon that others might not.

"Did so," Melonhead said then shot a left hook my way. His reach was longer than I'd guessed and he actually managed to hit my Yankees cap off my head. If only school lessons could be that quick and short.

I retreated to a more respectful distance and adjusted my attitude at the same time. "So exactly where'd you see them?"

"They're in the bike shop, in the basement where that old dummy lives. I seen them while I was down there and Uncle Billy had to go to the garage to get a new wheel. I picked out an *Outdoor Life* and there they was, three of them. Naked women and none was as big and hairy as Irma. She looks more like one of the bears in *Outdoor Life*. That's how I know."

That settled it. He knew and had instructed us with the facts. Melonhead was gloating that he had seen the real thing and we were left with our shabby recollections of the poor snoring soul in her unmade bed. We'd have to take the challenge and see those pictures to redeem our spirits if we stood a chance of realizing manhood, however distant that dream was.

As the four of us watched the sun settle behind the hills, our friend gave a detailed account of what he'd seen. I've spent the last thirty years as a cop and have heard my share and then some of lies and outrageous lies. Even today, as I make my assessment, Melonhead was telling the truth. He'd seen the pictures. The best I'd been able to do until the apple tree adventure, was view some topless women from Africa. Not often but a couple of times at the barbershop, the *National Geographic* had pictures which if you studied them, and I did, you could make out naked young girls. It wasn't much but in Mandan, North Dakota, in the 50's, it was the best a young boy could hope for. Until now when old fathead had pointed us to the mother lode and it was in a relative's basement right across First Avenue from my very own home.

If we cared to eat dinner, it was in our best interest to hurry home. There'd be no eating after the dishes were cleared. One at a time, we crawled out of our retreat and marched down the dirt path listening carefully for rattles. We hit the broken concrete sidewalk and talk moved to Halloween.

"I'm going as a ghost," Willie announced.

"You mean you're going as a kid hiding under an old sheet, just like last year," Mickey whispered to me to avoid offending our friend.

"And the year before, and the year before," I added. "I'm going as a hobo."

"Same as last year. Your clothes are so crappy, you won't need any costume," Willie retorted.

"Will too," I countered. "I have a pole with a handkerchief tied on the end to make it look real."

"Oh, yeah," Melonhead said sarcastically. "Only the best bums walk down the tracks carrying their snotrags on a pole."

"Mom said they used to. She said that when she was young, the hobos had her mom's house marked with blood or something cuz they were known as generous people. They'd give them food and the hobos would put it in the hankies tied to sticks."

The argument continued until it was time to split up, each to our own home. I turned left at Elm, and could see the lights on in our kitchen. I quickened the pace, but it was like running across a battlefield. The street next to the house was dug up again. Every summer the city workers gouged huge trenches to fix the road or whatever was broken below it. It took most of the summer, but to our joy and our parents' dismay they left piles of dirt and rocks which were either the makings of a fort or a traffic hazard depending upon which view you endorsed. Even better for us kids, the workers would mark their unfinished business with flaming round oil lamps placed on the street to warn drivers of the big hole that wasn't there in the spring. The lit lamps attracted kids like flies to a barn light. Once the forts were constructed it was a simple task to spill the oil and start our own fires much the same as any marauding invaders would do in the movies.

Tonight I didn't have time for forts or rudimentary pyrotechnics. That could wait till after I ate. I'd just about reached the fence gate when I heard a motorcycle approach rapidly. That was a rare sound unless it was Old Paddywacker, which it was.

"Hey kid," Paddywacker yelled as he slid to a stop on the loose dirt we'd kicked into the street. "Stop there, I want to talk to you about today." Paddywacker and I often had conversations. Sometimes about the neighbors' apple trees, sometimes about being out past curfew, but never, "Hey kid, how ya doing," or anything approaching civility or neighborliness. In fact, while he may have known my name, he never used it preferring 'boy' or 'kid.' Officer Paddywacker was a big man, almost as wide as tall. He always looked crumpled like he'd slept in the grey uniform that was thread bare. I know he ate all of his meals in uniform because the stains were testimony to what he'd consumed the last few days. I know he disliked dogs even though a careful study of his craggy face could lead one to believe he was part bulldog. He eased his substantial body off the tricycle, "Stop there, I want to talk to you about today."

Ah...busted...and for what? Maybe Irma had been watching us and called the cops on us. They had before when we used their little cottage to play Eeny-Einy-Over. We only used it because they had the smallest house on the block so it was easy to throw the ball over and even easier to run around after the ball was caught. I doubt if Frenchie would have called, he'd have taken care the matter on his own, with a dull knife.

"We didn't see anything, honest, we didn't see nothing." I thought I would get a denial out before he could start to dress me down.

"I don't know what you're talking about kid."

That threw me off guard.

"That damn dog of yours was chasing my cycle again. She bit at my leg and tore my pants– look!" He kicked his leg out and sure enough the pants were ripped.

So it was the dog that was in trouble. I chose to remain silent. Long before Miranda, I recognized that other than an outright denial, nothing good could come of talking to the likes of Paddywacker.

"Listen Sonny, if that pint-sized mutt of yours chases my scooter again, she's as good as in hound dog hell." He patted his aged six-shooter as proof of his intent. "You tell your parents that, too. You tell them to keep that dog on a chain or in your yard. And she needs a license, too, or it will be a life-sentence in the city pound—a short life sentence. You tell your Old Man that, Sonny." He turned away and mounted the three-wheeled scooter like Hop-A-Long himself. He kick started the machine and spun out on the loose rocks on a mission – likely to give more parking tickets, an enterprise doubtlessly fraught with even greater peril than his work as self-appointed dog-catcher.

Relieved that it was the family dog in trouble, I turned from tribulation and opened the gate to sanctuary. As though she'd overheard the exchange between me and the worthy constable, Duchess, the pint-sized mutt herself flew past me in hot pursuit of Old Paddywacker who fortuitously had already put some distance between them. Evidently, she was destined to live another day. Maybe longer since typically Old Paddywacker seldom came past our house and no one ever parked on our street in a bygone era when everyone had a garage with only the most pretentious or wealthy needing shelter for more than one car. He found it much easier posting tickets on the ranchers' pickups. They seldom cared to obey the parking rules when they came to town.

I slipped in the back door trying to refocus on my role in a house that included Mom and my brother, Mike, who were already at the table. The Old Man wouldn't be home until midnight when his shift as a trainman ended. Years later, when the railroad laid-off a few dozen men, he became a peace officer but not the kind that calls you 'boy.'

"Who was yelling out there?" Mom tuned in quickly. She had hearing like an owl…what would have been a distant point of white noise for any-one else, occurred to her as barnyard cacophony.

I told her about my encounter with the officer, pleased that it wasn't me in hot water and happy to represent that as the only event of the evening worth mentioning.

"You boys respect the police. But I never liked that man, Paddywacker. When I was nursing at the hospital, he filled the emergency ward every Saturday night with broken heads. He didn't have to beat on those poor drunk souls. If a stout, sober man stood up to him, Paddywacker would be on that tricycle of his like a fly to dog poop."

We'd heard that story a dozen times. Mom had been a nurse at the local hospital and she didn't take kindly to having to mend fractured heads. She told us that she'd even complained to the Chief of Police, but reprimanding Paddywacker might require the Chief to actually leave the station where he vigilantly guarded a cell that was empty six days a week.

"Now, you boys finish eating and then let's get your Halloween costumes ready. The big day is tomorrow," she reminded us with an enthusiasm for costumes that exceeded that of any kid.

We, in fact, had no need to be reminded that Halloween was on its way just as sure as candy in the bag. October 31st to us was the biggest day of the year. There were the treats without the Christmas blizzards; the costumes worn by us instead of stale-breathed store Santas and no lines to remember for the Christmas pageant. How could you blow the line, 'Trick or Treat?' And no worries about being good during a celebration that actually rewarded the threat of a little mischief.

Under the hand sewn patchwork quilts of our beds, my brother and I were safe from parental oversight of the day's events. I told him about Irma, my brush with death, and the revelation that Uncle Billy held a stash of magazines that would be roughly equal to finding the end of the rainbow.

He, being two years older, listened to WLS on the small transistor radio and pretended not to be interested. However, I knew he was. I could see it in his eyes.

My brother was notoriously competitive but annoyingly talented and he always had to top my stories – no easy task in this matter. He moved the little red radio away from his ear and sat up. "The Gypsies are in town."

"They are?! Where'd you see them? Melonhead didn't say nothing about that."

"Melonhead wouldn't know his asshole from a knothole," a phrase my brother had sagely palmed from my father. "I saw a whole bunch of them when I was coming home from football…they're down at the park, along the cemetery, where they always camp."

It shouldn't have been a surprise. They came every year just like Santa and the Easter Bunny – a regular part of our calendar. And every year, my mother warned us to stay away from the camp. She never offered much of a reason, but Melonhead filled in that bit of information. Seems the Gypsies were given to taking young children with them when they left town. Of course, armed with that threat, every year we spent hours laying behind the dike and watching the little band of trailers and dark-skinned families going about their business. At times, fiddle and guitar music would drift our way with strange melodies, or non-melodies that only served to pique our interests.

Back in the familiar terrain of my own bed, Gypsies, Irma, Frenchie, Paddywacker, Uncle Billy's magazine, and Halloween all blended together in my imagination as I tried to sleep. From my brother's transistor The Coasters sang "Poison Ivy" in tiny voices as a cool breeze carrying the pleasant aroma of dried leaves drifted through the partially open window. Sleep came but not easily.

The smell of bacon and waffles roused me from my slumber. Pots and pans clanged in the kitchen. The sheets had twisted around my body and my pillow had gone to the hardwood floor. It had been a restless sleep and I had a vague sense of being harassed by a cast of villains—some I recognized from the movies, some from television, and some from my own store of demons. Dad had shut my window at some point and must have also turned Mike's radio off during his evening rounds to close down the house after another day. The steam pipes banged and the heat from the radiator next to my bed warmed my bare toes. Halloween, it was Halloween, the thought hit me and the excitement brought me to my feet. The floor was cold and I quickly dressed in yesterday's jeans and my old Gene Autry sweatshirt. I flew down the stairs to the kitchen. The Old Man was up already and reading the paper with his coffee cup in hand. He didn't look at me, but said, "Saw Frenchie at the Legion last night. Said you boys were in his apple tree. Stay out of his yard. He's not a man to be crossing. And try to remember that it's not easy to make a get-away when you're up in a tree."

The Old Man knew of men such as Frenchie or so I imagined. He, himself, was a combat veteran who had driven a half-track across Europe, most often at night without the benefit of tell-tale headlights. He never spoke of such things to us boys, but I'd hear him talk sparingly to his buddies sometimes when they were enjoying a beer in the garage. And we found the Twelfth Armored Division commemorative book. Burned bodies of Nazis and blown up tanks were enough to convince me that the Old Man knew what he was talking about.

"We will." I'd learned already to spread the guilt around with a 'we.' Being the youngest in the neighborhood it gave me an opportunity to hint that perhaps I'd just been led astray by the others.

My mother curtailed any chance of further inquisition when she appeared at the table with a brown paper grocery bag. "Here's your costume for school…and your treats to share with the class." I grabbed the bag with the hand that wasn't clutching the bacon and peered in. Homemade cookies, chocolate chip, wrapped in cellophane paper, lay on top of my clothes, a torn and patched shirt and jeans and a handkerchief rolled in a bundle stuffed with newspaper.

"Where's my stick?"

"On the back porch. Take it when you leave. And you'd best get goin' now."

I grabbed a couple more strips of bacon, finished my milk, and raced out the door to join all the other ghosts and goblins in their heathen revelry.

"Don't let the dog out of the gate and Mikey says the Gypsies are in town, so you stay away…"

I dashed up the hill, past the white church, past the Goldberg mansion, past the back of Snake Hill and to the playground. I paused just long enough to help myself to a couple of cookies while I rested on the merry-go-round then off to the classroom. Miss Martin stood at the door and greeted each of us. Miss Martin, the love of my life. She was all a boy could hope for and when she bent down and gave each of us a hug, her perfume stayed with me for the day, and my feet didn't need to touch the floor as I moved to my desk. Miss Martin!

Reading, arithmetic, spelling…we covered them all but nothing stuck as it was the Halloween party after lunch and second recess that mattered.

Finally, the clock's hands moved to two and the party was on. We were dismissed to attend to our costumes. Some went to the rest room to change, but mostly we just pulled the attire from our bags and put them on over our clothes. I struggled, but when I finally stood, my tattered jeans, flannel shirt, a holey pair of the Old Man's dress shoes, and of course, my hobo's stick looked pretty good as I modeled in front of the full length mirror in the back of the room. I added some black Crayon to my rosy cheeks to simulate the smudge I seemed to remember on the faces of most hobos I'd seen. Miss Martin soon clapped her hands and directed us to the hallway to join the parade.

Ghosts, princesses, scarecrows, cowboys and cowgirls, and a motley flock of other 'itinerates' soon joined the witches and goblins in the grand parade down the hallway, twice around, and then back to the classroom where mothers with treats and red punch waited for us. Then the bell rang and I hustled past Miss Martin, but she grabbed my shoulder and pulled me back. "Here's a note to your mother, don't forget to give it to her." She smoothed my cowlick and patted me away. I crushed the note into my hobo pants and ran to catch up with the others. "Don't run," every adult shouted. Don't run? They had no sense of the importance of the matter. Don't run from a burning building or a rattling snake?

Mike, Willie, Mickey, and of course, Melonhead were already assembled in the back yard under the chokecherry tree when I arrived. Daylight was burning and plans needed to be made, although it was never clear to me why. We had the same plan every year. Start at Aunt Cora's house. Hit the 'rich' people up on Goldberg's hill, then move to Uncle Herman's little Dutch Colonial, and end up with a full grocery bag of candy. That was capped off by the unprofitable but perfunctory stop at the home of Aunt Tillie and Uncle Bill…unprofitable until this year.

That was the same route we used every Halloween. But this year the older boys had an addition to the plan. They went over it for my benefit then we split up agreeing to meet at sunset by the oil lamps. Mike and I had just enough time to ride the rusty bikes Uncle Bill had made from spare parts, down to the dike. We hit the alleys and made our way over the viaduct sheltering Gypsies, trolls, and the hobos cooking underneath. What a life those tramps had. Other than maybe a cowboy, I thought the life of a bum was truly something to aspire to. Surely the current Miss Martin and my future wife would see the wisdom in making friends with the musically inclined Gypsies and the world-travelling hobos encumbered only by a stick and hanky.

We arrived at the dike dumping our bikes along the banks of the chocolate colored Cannonball River. We crawled to the top and there they were – maybe a dozen pickups, a few trailers in a circle and three horse trailers.

Proud buckskin and white paint horses grazed on the park lawn. The Gypsies already had a large fire burning in the center of the encampment. It was their little kingdom down there. Be a tough choice, Gypsy, hobo, or cowboy. A thought fluttered through my mind. Maybe I should join up. But not on this night – it was Halloween and we had our own little kingdom to plunder. Didn't look like the Gypsy kids would be trick or treating although it was the one night it would be a challenge to sort out who was a true Gypsy and who was trying it out just for the occasion. We mounted our standard issue, one-gear bikes that we supposed would be the model kids would ride forever. As we rode back over the bridge, I looked again at the hobos' great bonfire and I smelled the burning wood as we passed overhead. Who knew what magical spells and incantations they were brewing down there in Sterno cans especially with the Gypsies available as consultants.

If we ate dinner, I don't recall. But I do remember we were the first to the oil lamps. A slight breeze caused the lamps to flicker and carried the redolence of burning leaves to our noses. I lay back on the dirt pile and watched the stars slowly appear. I felt a rough kick to my butt. Melonhead had arrived. If he hadn't kicked me, I wouldn't have known it was he. On his head, he wore a pumpkin that formed an exact circle on his shoulders…a very big circle, but exact. The eyes were neatly carved and the circle was broken by the same mean, gap-toothed smile he normally entertained the world with. I was tempted to inquire about the process through which he affixed the pumpkin shell so precisely to his head but suspected that would provoke him into booting me again with a precision that ought not to belong to a kid with a gourd over his head. Forgoing curiosity and valor, I jumped up and grabbed my stick.

True to his word, Willie appeared as a kid with a sheet. Mickey exploited his natural resemblance to a happy chimp by just adding whiskers to his smile with eyeliner. The shock value in this simple but brilliant ensemble was added by a shrunken head dangling below the benevolent smile on dirty twine. It seemed out of place suspended around Mickey's monk-like visage and it spooked me out every time I saw him wear it. I was all for being frightened on this one special evening but not with that kind of scariness. Mike was a millionaire, something none of us had ever seen or been near so that left the door open for artistic interpretation. He had a straw hat with play money stuffed around the hatband. Hard to imagine that rich folks walked around like that, but as I said none of us had ever seen one so who were we to question? Mike led the way which was good because I doubt if Melonhead was up to the task on this night.

"Trick or Treat, Trick or Treat," we shouted at every door until our voices were hoarse. The bags filled, we made an appropriate number of rest stops to trade candy and eat our fill. Melonhead hadn't calculated how he was going to feed his pumpkin, but being ever so resourceful in all matters of eating, dining, or grazing, he ordered Willie to push candy through the Pumpkin grin into his mouth–awkward, but filling.

Finally, bags nearly ripping from the weight, we made our way to Aunt Tillie and Uncle Bill's place. It was a lovely two story prairie style home. A white porch with rockers filled the front. Light filled every window, except the upstairs which she rented out to railroad men resting between train rides. A couple of fairies and a cowboy were at the porch so we respectfully waited until they had their turn.

"It's Aunt Tillie who's handing out the candy," Mike said.

"She always does. Uncle Billy can't hear the kids when they shout."

"Okay, boys this is it. Put the plan to action," Mike ordered.

Mike led Willie, Mickey, and the Pumpkin up the steps. They pounded at the door. "Trick or Treat!" Aunt Tillie, wearing her trademark white pearl necklace, red lipstick, and print dress, greeted the boys with a twinkle in her eye. "Oh my, what do we have here? Let me see, a ghost, a monkey or a cat with a shrunken head, my, that looks real, a pumpkin and my, Mikey what are you?"

"Rich. Is Uncle Billy, here? We have something for him."

"No tricks…"

"No, we were just going to give him a present, you know, 'cause he made our bikes for us and all…" Mike stammered with an uncertainty that made me wonder if I should be more worried than I was.

"Wait here, but no tricks, no burning poop bags like you boys did two years ago. He's still fussing about that." Aunt Tillie retreated into the abode. I made my way to the back of the house and Willie the ghost moved off the porch to the side, just like our plan. I was getting nervous. It was taking too long. I rested my stick on the house and sat on the rusty metal garden bench to wait. I rehearsed my part in my mind. Then a clump of dirt came flying my way from a ghost momentarily possessed of a small but quick arm. A signal, I suppose. I shot up and around the corner, up the back steps and into the kitchen. Just like I'd rehearsed, down the worn steps and into the bowels of the dank basement – bike parts everywhere – smelled of oil and grease. I'd hoped the magazines hadn't been moved as I slipped past the parts. On the table, *Outdoor Life*, just like Melonhead had said. I lifted the magazine and looked at the next one, *Sports Afield*. The next, *Look*, and then *Life*, and then the mother lode, the prettiest blonde woman, large smile, a slinky black dress, and waving–to me, I guess. Even in the dim light, I could read, 'Marilyn Monroe, Nude.' I slipped the treasure into my flannel hobo shirt and started my escape. Then steps, heavy steps, the kind Frankenstein made as he escaped from the castle, on the kitchen floor stopped my getaway.

I jumped off the steps and scurried under them just as Uncle Billy made his way down. I could see his weathered scuffed work boots go past as I held my breath and hugged Marilyn closer to my heart. It was as though she'd been trapped in Uncle Billy's basement and when she saw me, the biggest smile and the wave, I was here to free her. I could feel my heart thumping. Had Uncle Billy been able to hear, he'd found me from the thump, thump, thump. That and I knocked over a bucket of sprockets as I backed from the steps. He tottered to the magazines. He lifted the *Outdoor Life*, the *Sports Afield*, the *Look*, and then settled on *Life*. He strolled off to his bedroom in the corner, eating a candy bar as he paged through the magazine. Marilyn and I were going to make it…as long as the boys kept Aunt Tillie busy at the door. I crept up the stairs and into the kitchen. It smelled of fried donuts. They lay on the table and I helped myself to one as I passed by. Then it was out the door and freedom for us both.

Suddenly it dawned on me, the ghost, the monkey with the shrunken head, the pumpkin head, and the millionaire, they'd want to share. Greed and jealousy overwhelmed my soul. I paused on the garden bench and removed the magazine from my shirt. I stared at the cover and hesitated to explore beyond. Would it be as Melonhead had painstakingly described? Would it be even better? For the briefest time, I entertained a thought that on those inside pages, she'd look like Irma. But, no, no one would buy a magazine to look at that. I slowly pulled the cover back. It opened to a page that had been marked with a dog ear and use. Even in the poor light from the window above, I knew there was a future. I knew that all womanhood wasn't like my naked neighbor. I was stunned and yet hopeful – until the others joined me. Mike grabbed my prize from my cold hands. Life was going to be like that.

We meandered back towards Melonhead's house, waving to Old Paddywacker as he drove under the streetlight on his tricycle. He scowled and sped away. Melonhead stopped under the streetlight to spend some time with her. Mike and I settled next to him in a pile of crunchy leaves and began inventory of our stash of candies. Willie and Mickey continued on home to drop their bags off. There was talk of going out again although our curfew time was drawing near. The ten o'clock siren would announce that soon. "An apple, someone dropped an apple in my bag." Mike pulled out a shiny big one.

"Was probably the Elmer's trying to show off," Melonhead said not looking up from the pages which shone glossy under the streetlight.

"One year, I got a hundred and sixty-seven oranges," I tossed out. When the assertion drew no response I boldly added a concession, "I gave them away." I moved closer to Melonhead and looked over his shoulder. Life was going to be good!

Willie, still wearing his white sheet, arrived back unexpectedly with a screeching stop. He was breathing hard. "There's a bunch of Gypsy kids coming down the sidewalk." He pointed back over his shoulder. Mickey returned clutching his bag. As though he was seeing the universe unfold from its beginnings, Mickey repeated, "There's a bunch of Gypsy kids coming down the sidewalk."

We all stood and watched. There were five or six. All about our size. They were dressed like Gypsies which is to say they didn't wear costumes. Maybe last year they'd all been just kids like us. Kids who hadn't listened to their parents and were stolen away. I really wanted to ask them what it was like.

"Look, Old Paddywacker on his scooter," Mike pointed down the road. He was coming back towards us but stopped at the Gypsy kids. We could hear him yell at the kids to get home – to get out of the neighborhood. The kids stood their ground as he approached. They gave no quarter until he dismounted and he went for the wooden stick clipped to his duty belt. A couple of swings in the air by the leather lanyard like a Kung Fu champion and they backed away.

Melonhead respectfully lay the magazine down on the leaves. "Take off your costume, Moose, fast."

"No, are you…"

He was an impatient sort and began to do the job himself. I pushed him back and finished taking the flannel shirt off. I handed it to him. He dropped to his knees and began to fill the buttoned shirt with leaves, first the sleeves and then the body. I gave him my hobo pants and he resumed stuffing. When he was done, he tied the shirt tails to the belt loop and held it up for approval.

"Hide," Melonhead commanded and we did. Before jumping, I rescued Marilyn for the second time this night and then joined my brother in the construction ditch. It was dark but for the flickering oil lamps we could see when we looked skyward. Melonhead handed down the stuffed hobo to my brother.

"What are you doing?" Mike asked.

"Watch." Melonhead dragging the hobo crawled out of the ditch and slithered behind a pile of dirt.

I could hear Old Paddywacker's scooter purring along nearer and nearer. Just as it was beside us, Melonhead stood from behind the dirt mound and tossed the hobo into the scooter's headlights. The police officer let out a terrible wail, louder and more ominous than the patrol car sirens. Looking up, I saw him flying across the top of the narrow ditch.

I stuck my head up over the top and saw the rotund officer make an amazing two point landing. The scooter was on its side and still running. Melonhead slipped back down beside us. It could have been bad for the three of us in the hole, but for Willie and Mickey who had been hiding in the hedge along the sidewalk. Those two were fast. Willie made a break to the right, his sheets flying off as he ran. Mickey made a move to the left, his shrunken head swinging to his back. Old Paddywacker started after Willie but then broke for Mickey. That indecision cost the officer an arrest that night. Like a tight end who gets the extra step on the defender, Mickey high stepped across the street and vanished into the blackness. The cursing officer gave chase waving his stick over his head. He had disappeared into the abyss. When Mickey needed to disappear, he could.

Melonhead, ever the capable strategist, recognized the opportunity and issued his simple order. "Run."

We did, I clawed my way over the top like some Doughboy charging the Krauts. We made it to our garage and to the safety of the chokecherry tree. We shinnied up the tree and onto the garage roof. We'd learned long ago to take the high ground. Silently, we watched as Old Paddywacker returned. He was panting and beating the stick into his hand, cursing. He righted the scooter with superhuman strength and much anger, mounted the machine, and drove off. It looked to us as though the front wheel had been bent as it wobbled. He left and the rain, actually more of a sleet, came down hard and fast. We stood our ground, or roof, as it was because our leader thought it too early to get down.

He was right. Old Paddywacker had driven around the block and now without lights was cruising past. We waited for some time, enough to be thoroughly drenched when we came through the back door and into the kitchen. Fortunately, Mom was in the front room with Aunt Tillie. We were able to slip upstairs and crawl into bed. It was a fitful night sleep fired by sugar and filled with visions of Marilyn not to mention the chase.

The note! That was my waking thought. Miss Martin's note to my mother. It was in my hobo pants that Melonhead threw in front of the police scooter. I jumped out of bed and ran to the window. We were likely surrounded by police cars. None. They hadn't found the note, not yet.

I shook my brother awake and told him my fear. He sat up for a moment. "Did you look outside to see if he even took the pants?" Then he laid back and covered his head with a pillow.

I will say my brother had some insights, likely due to his advanced age. I dressed and scrambled down the second story back steps avoiding the kitchen entirely. The skies had cleared and the air was fresh and cool. There was hope. I dashed through the back yard, past the open gate, and to the ditch. The oil lamps had burned out. I saw no clothes. I tiptoed to the edge. Candy and two half eaten apples littered the dirt mound. There on the bottom lay my hobo pants, no shirt but the pants, more candy and Marilyn. Like my pants, she was covered with mud. Still she smiled and waved up to me. I gave her a little wave back then took my hobo stick and fished out the pants from the muddy water. The note, albeit soggy, was still in the pocket.

I stood looking down at the pretty woman with the big smile. I thought about fishing her out. It just won't be the same after all we'd been through together. And then she ends up in the filthy water. She'd never be the same if I brought her up. I decided to remember her the way she was when we first met and to this day, I haven't forgotten.

SNOWBALLS

On the bulletin board the ghosts and witches had come down
replaced by pilgrims with tall hats and glum faces sharing a feast with the smiling Indians, so it was no surprise when I saw large white flakes gently drifting outside the classroom window. I turned in my desk chair and whispered the magic word to Mickey, "Snowww…" Evidently my enthusiasm amplified my voice since Miss Martin interrupted an inspired lecture on Plymouth Rock to glance out the window causing everyone in the class to rise on tiptoes.

"Settle down, please, you've all seen snow before," she scolded gently. She looked through her dark framed glasses directly at me. I could feel the embarrassment spreading like some childhood illness that stopped just short of me wanting to disappear.

She returned to her lesson and I to my reverie – the spell had been cast – my mind had been lassoed and dragged out into the white playground. Snowmen, snowballs, and snow angels all awaited us. Ten minutes and we'd be turned out for recess into a schoolyard that provided more entertainment than the bottom of a Christmas tree.

The bell clanged and without waiting for further instructions, I extricated myself from the wooden desk that had subjugated generations of scholars before me and dashed to my locker. I grabbed my corduroy coat and rushed past Miss Martin.

"No snowballs, boys."

Quickly putting that warning aside, the only obstacle to my favorite winter sport would be bad snow. To the Old Man any snow was bad snow, but to us it was the stuff that was so cold and so dry that it couldn't be packed into the hard round balls necessary for good aim and optimal impact. Bad snow was as worthless as the fool's gold littering Snake Hill. But the first snow of the year seldom yielded bad snow… the first snow was Mother Nature's building blocks, her gift to kids. It was normally the prime stuff of the season as it fell when the temperature was just perfect, a bit below slush and a lot above fluff.

A rush of cold fresh air greeted me as I cleared the double door held opened by the janitors, Senior and Junior. Father and son, they looked alike, walked alike, dressed alike, and even smelled the same, a musky odor of accumulated sweat produced by manual labor. I had asked my mother, who was the school nurse, about the soiled attire and she said the family was poor and didn't have running water at their house. We prayed for their dirty uniforms that night and for enough running water for all families short of a flash flood.

A few other classes had beaten us to the hill behind the school. They'd already taken the cardboard boxes that Senior and Junior had stacked to be burned and were laying down a sliding slope that would be as smooth and clear as crystal by Christmas. I saw this on the run and knew there was no point wasting time waiting for a turn. That would come. I made a bee-line to the merry-go-round and lunged at the only open space. I landed hard and clutched the cold metal bars with bare hands. Older boys took turns spinning the ride faster and faster. The snow and ice on the floor made it impossible to stand or sit. We clung to each other and laid flat on our stomachs until one by one we surrendered to fatigue and were cast off by centrifugal force to the frozen pea rock. The elders laughed at each youngster they forced to the ground. Yet they always had an eager new contestant certain he or she would be the first to still be hanging on when the bell rang or the older boys realized they were doing all the work.

"Moose, over here, please," came a plea from on high.

I turned and saw that Mickey, a wisp of a boy with a face that I would now liken to a smiling Buddhist monk, was in the air at the end of the see-saw. A little girl in front of Mickey screamed for her life. Three younger boys and a chubby girl with a mean face had jumped on the other end and were whipping my friend up and down like he was on the failing tail end of an eight second bull ride. Instinctively, I ran to his aid. Timing was everything. When the board reached a reasonable height on the downward motion, I would leap on. My vertical jump was about three inches in a new pair of tennis shoes. But then, a tactical mistake on their part. Perfect, they'd lowered Mickey to within my limited range and I was on the back. The momentum of the game swung. Two of the boys fell off when my weight brought us suddenly to the ground. The girl tightened her grip on the metal bar and the other boy wrapped his arms around her. Without saying a word, we bailed. The two crashed to the ground in a yelping tangle of arms, legs and bodies attired in over-stuffed winter suits. To add an exclamation mark to our triumph, we each scooped up a fist full of snow and tossed it above the group to make a shower of crystal that created fleeting rainbows of color.

"Come on there's cardboard."

Slipping and sliding, we made our way across the playground to the base of the hill. Cardboard was piling up quickly as the race down the hill was sorting out those who thought they wanted to go fast from those who couldn't go fast enough. The hill was steep and with so little snow on the bottom, landings could be cruel. Some limped away. Some just sat or lay on the ground like victims of a natural gas explosion trying to get their wits about them. Mickey beat me up the hill with an extra wide box. I never actually saw him run up the hill. He was at the bottom then the top. He was like that. He waited patiently and I arrived panting.

"Front or back?" he asked as though holding open the door to a limousine for me.

"Front."

There were advantages to both seats. The front offered the best view going down. The back offered a cushion in the form of the driver in the event that ride came to an unexpected stop. I'd seen this happen when a slight rise in the slide caused a couple of riders to career off the trail right into the monkey bars where the driver was wedged like a cork in a barrel. I wanted the view and knew my slight friend wouldn't offer much protection anyway.

In the fashion of Olympic bobsledders, we ran beside the ragged, flattened box until we got to the beginning of the run and jumped on. No steering, no brakes, no helmets, just the rush of wind causing our eyes to tear as we screamed our way over the polished snow.

In the distance, a bell announced the end of recess and what should have been the end of our run. Not a reliable conveyance, the cardboard stopped when we hit a patch of dry concrete. We continued on our own right up to the side of the enormous barrel where Senior and Junior burned whatever it was the school needed to be rid of. Mickey had clutched my waist the entire time. I stood and shook him off. He fell to his back and looked at me with a smile that said, 'If you know how it's going to turn out, it's just a trip not an adventure...'

If recess had been a full hour, I wouldn't have lived to be eleven—adventures with Mickey were like that. We dusted off the snow from our jackets, and limped into the old brick building. Father and son held the doors open and occasionally sent students off to the side. Junior relinquished his door post and roughly broomed the snow from kids who failed to pass the entrance inspection.

I'm sure Miss Martin offered up compelling lessons on the addition of apples and oranges or the intriguing adventures of Dick and Jane, although I was elsewhere....my mind wandered away from Miss Martin and the book in front of me out through the window, past the rigors and rituals of school curriculum and into the air with Chuck Yeager on the tail of a Luftwaffe fighter plane. I was his wingman and an ace myself if one counted the number I personally shot down during those flights out of the classroom. I spent the remainder of the afternoon in the wild blue yonder and was finally brought back to Earth with the last bell of the day. It had been tough flying today in the snow.

Back out the double doors a third time and under the watchful gaze of the janitors, I met up with Mickey, Willie, and my brother Mike. It was understood that a snowball fight would begin the instant we left the schoolyard and soon a running battle was underway. There were no sides, everyone was a fair target. I ran from tree to fence packing balls together as I sought shelter from the incoming. The snow was as good as I could remember, there was plenty of it and it was all free for the taking. How, I wondered, could it be that grown-ups had neglected to assert dominion over this wonderland the way they had in most areas of a kid's life. It was amazing that no one had thought to box and sell this stuff—at least not up until they began making the fake snow, fake trees and fake Christmas carols (which included "Blue, Blue Christmas" and everything after).

I'd gotten a start in the snow business, like most, with snowmen. Mom, who hadn't forgotten how to be a kid, even freed up a carrot or two for noses and we'd drag old clothes out to dress the plump men. Once, we appropriated the Old Man's Sunday hat. A unique and colorful tapestry of curses, questions, and commentary issued from the deepest recess of my father's chest when he saw old Frosty adorned with his fedora. The man had a gift for expression, but Frosty had his hat.

It wasn't a great leap of imagination to picture a miniature version of the snowman's head as a projectile that could cover vast expanses to avenge or antagonize the target of the day...or even just satisfy the need for symmetry afforded by the simple act of aiming, throwing and hitting. Such was our appreciation for the aesthetics that it couldn't be sated by snowball fights alone, however. No, this was recreation elevated to the status of outdoor sport and it required rules. Not written or even spoken, just hammered out on the anvil of hard experience, sometimes with fists, over the years and passed on in the tradition of all great cultural legends. According to these dictums, one couldn't fire a shot straight into the face of the adversary…if a bad throw resulted in someone being hit in the face, such were the risks in playing in a high-stakes game, still it should be expected that the next missile headed your way would also be the result of a throwing error. There were no "ice balls" allowed unless you were Eddie Goldberg or were throwing at Eddie Goldberg. It was deemed cowardly to hit a fleeing adversary in the back unless he had broken any of the other rules. The main rule about girls was that you can throw in the general direction where they stood, meaning north rather than south, but any closer and they would tell. Besides there were body parts to girls that were way off limits and to hit any of those areas was to bring your intentions well into the realm of suspicion. These were the rules and violations were handled with fists and headlocks even if that meant waiting until the Fourth of July.

So, we 'expanded our horizons.' A platitude first espoused by Miss Martin although I believe she offered it as a reason to learn the musical scales and the difference between a quarter note and a quarter horse. We expanded into moving targets: cars, trucks, and trains. Anything that moved presented a challenge that was met with a loud 'clunk' on the metal roof, hood, or trailer panel. It was a pleasant and less violent pastime. Instead of fighting we tended to admire each other's ability to make the long shot. A few were even unforgettable, like the time Melonhead tossed his notorious 'Melonball' at the semi-tractor trailer and missed. How could you miss a semi trailer? Even more remarkable was that Old Paddywacker was trailing behind the truck on his three-wheeled scooter and took the hit on his windshield. That resulted in a remarkable chase that landed Melonhead in juvenile court. Fortunately, it was March and near the end of the season so ceasing our activities in deference to his sentence wasn't too painful.

There was more to the sport than lobbing balls. It was more than spring training for Little League. At first, that was all there was. However, experience taught that strategy, planning, and running were essential elements especially if one had intentions of a long career. Melonhead's unfortunate encounter with the law taught us that, as he hadn't planned an escape route and that oversight coupled with his sloth-like speed was the reason he was getting a free ride in the squad car even before his snowball melted off Pad-dywacker's windshield.

On this first night of snow, field conditions were good. Over six inches of wet snow had accumulated. A near perfect ball could be formed with a single squeeze. It was warm and gloves were optional. Clouds covered the full moon affording us dark alleys and corners. Traffic, especially the semi-tractors, was slowed because of the slippery road. We set off to a favorite place of ambush, the dark space between the Mobil station and Ohm's ham-burger joint – just wide enough for us to stand three abreast and in two rows. The road was steep and there were no street lights.

We could have walked to Ohm's, it was only two blocks, but the icy streets provided an alternative form of transportation. Intersections with stop signs were like bus stops. When the cars would stop, one or two of us would scurry out of cover and grab the chrome. Studebakers, I recall, had excep-tionally big rear bumpers to clutch and squat. They seemed to be owned by folks with hats who drove slowly, so I favored them.

We gathered behind the café after our rides unwittingly delivered us to our destination. Except Mickey, his four-door Dodge sedan had made an unexpected turn then a second at a speed too great for him to let go. He caught up to me a bit later with a knee torn from his jeans and a story to tell. Seems the Dodge was driven by some duck-tailed hoods who knew that he was on their bumper and gave him a long and terrifying ride. I wasn't there, however, in my mind I could see the smile on his face even in the face of death by bumpershining. He was a boy to whom fear was a complete stranger; if he had met fear, though, I suspect he would have smiled, put an arm around it and asked gently why it wanted to cause so much misery.

We'd already picked off a few trailers when Mickey joined us. We'd pretty much confined ourselves to trailers as our appetite for being chased by cars was diminishing since the year before when Eddie Goldberg cracked a windshield with an iceball then realized it was his own father on the other side of the glass. Truckers never stopped. I doubt they even knew they'd had a role in the script.

Sometimes we'd make exceptions and when a black Dodge sedan came poking up Main Street from the east, Mickey was sure it was the hoods. I called for everyone to blast the Dodge. We did. Five distinct booms rang out. Five for five. The Dodge slowed to a crawl and we prepared to escape in all directions expecting the leather clad teenagers to be following in hot pursuit.

It didn't quite happen that way. As expected the Dodge pulled curbside and stopped. The driver's door opened. We crouched and waited. The driver emerged, no shouting or threats. I'd hoped we weren't dealing with a character like the maniac, Norman Bates, in the movie "Psycho." The small figure in a long dark coat walked around the car and then looked our way. The headlights of an oncoming car illuminated her face. Miss Martin.

She took a step towards the café. And then another. I stood on the sidewalk. My hat was pulled down low and a scarf covered my face like a train robber. Then, our eyes met. And, I ran.

"Miss Martin phoned," my mother told me before bedtime prayers. It looked as though I would have a lot more praying to do than just blessing my parents, the dog, and the family cat.

What was the best gambit here? Feign ignorance? Pretend it was good news? Fess up? I could confess, toss in something about palming the nickel from my weekly donation to keep the church solvent, then repent and throw myself on her mercy. I'd watched my older brother in situations like this. He'd developed a technique of waiting. I asked him why and he said that there was no point in giving up too early. A few times after that lesson, he even pointed out scenes in movies where the actor would have fared better remaining mum. However, in this instance, Mom had laid the matter at my feet and it required a carefully calculated response.

"What did she want?" An inspired strategy.

"Oh, she just wondered if I would come in to your class and talk about personal hygiene. You know, I did that for your third grade class."

"That's all? That's all she wanted…stuff about my hygiene?"

"Not your hygiene in particular….why, what else should she want?"

I'd let impulse get the best of me. I'd broken Mike's rule to remain silent.

"No, I was just wondering if you are going to bring those big plastic teeth and that foot long toothbrush."

"Yes, I imagine I will. Why?" A nine out of ten on the doubt meter.

"We're getting kinda old for that, Mom. And the guys think we actually use that brush. Last time it took them a month before they stopped calling me Big Mouth."

"You're never too old to learn how to brush properly." Ah…she was back to hygiene. A good recovery. Hygiene was right behind the Lord on my mother's list of things to respect and talk about…right above me, my brother and my father. One of her earliest attempts at hygienic behavior modification was the use of a bathroom chart on which we placed a star next to our name each time we brushed our teeth…there was a prize for the winner and, although I can't now recall, it must have been attractive enough for my brother to buy his own box of stars. Within a week he had a line behind his name that would have stretched to the moon if it hadn't been so crooked. We had our very own constellation right above the bathroom sink. When my father observed with a hint of envy that Mike must have a dozen stars for every tooth he brushed rather than every time he brushed, the chart was taken down, the stars were confiscated and we did penance by having to brush with Colgate rather than the favored Stripe toothpaste that had won over children of every age.

For now, though, I was home free. Miss Martin hadn't recognized me. I added a silent word of appreciation for that after Mom finished asking the Lord to take my soul…something I wasn't ready to surrender quite yet.

. . . .

We were into the third hour of class and, more than the blackboard, I was studying Miss Martin's face and listening for any coded message she might be aiming at me. There were none. She looked as pure as the driven snow just like every other day.

It was after lunch that it started. With Arithmetic…the one subject I deemed to be void of any emotion, codes, or sub-plots.

"Now, class….please listen carefully. If a boy has twenty-three snowballs and throws, let me see, five, yes five of them, Larry how many snowballs does he have left?"

"None."

"None?"

"That's all he had. He didn't throw any more."

"Hmmmm….Mary, do you know?"

"Eighteen, Miss Martin. He'd have eighteen left."

"Very good, Mary. Now if a boy has thirty-six snowballs and throws eight of them at a passing car but misses three times, how many does he have left? Larry, do you want to try that one?"

"Twenty-Five?"

"Was that an answer or a question?"

"He shouldn't be throwing at cars," Mary said.

"No, he shouldn't Mary. You're right about that."

"I saw my brother do that one time and I told my father," Mary added as a proclamation of her virtue and a warning to evil-doers. The warning wasn't necessary. Everyone knew Mary was chronically compelled to snitch…she couldn't seem to help herself and that served her well later on as a free-lance gossiper for the local newspaper.

I couldn't steady my nerves or hold on to a thought for the rest of the class and was able to escape this paralysis only when I realized Mickey was standing next to my desk. "That wasn't so bad….it could have been a lot worse. She could have turned you into the police and Paddywacker would beat you with a rubber hose and put you in the hole. Then a judge would send you to the Reform School. She could have sent you to the principal and he could have beat on you with his special paddle that doesn't leave marks. Then he could have turned you over to your father for another paddling and he wouldn't care if he did leave marks. So come on…let's go, it's recess." I looked up into Mickey's smiling eyes, and suddenly realized the wisdom in his words—it was time for recess. I dumped my books into the desk well and scampered back to my locker. I pulled on the Mandan Braves sweatshirt that I'd helped myself from Mike's closet. I'd never wear that old corduroy coat to school again.

"Larry, you have a new coat?"

Only Miss Martin would notice and she did.

"Yes, Ma'am, it's my brother's."

She didn't reply, although I could imagine her eyes burning into my back as I turned and ran from her glare. I found Mickey and we tracked down Willie. We huddled behind the old trash burner. The warmth of the fire was the only thing that felt good.

"She knows. That's why she gave me those snowball questions."

"I don't think she saw me, 'cause she doesn't ask me any questions," Mickey said. That was understandable…it seemed like I was the only one who ever asked for his views.

Willie offered his perspective. "I think you're just making this stuff up. If she knew, she'd call your parents. She'd take you to the principal's office. She'd call the police. She'd…"

Willie's help wasn't helping. It only foreshadowed my fate. I stopped listening and turned away covering my ears.

"She's watching us. Look, through the principal's window. They're both looking right at us."

Willie looked then offered solace by assuring me that I was, indeed, 'crazy.' Maybe I was. Maybe it was just the guilt and shame that made me think this way. Maybe she didn't really know I'd thrown the snowballs. Willie had a good point. I knew one thing for sure: being a lying crook wasn't a career option for me. The anxiety alone was a jail cell.

When the bell sounded the end to recess, I only had a couple of hours to get through. I began to make promises to myself and the Lord about what I wouldn't do if He would just let me wiggle off the hook. I'd never make another snowball let alone throw one at a car or a human being except Eddie Goldberg. I wouldn't take the Lord's name in vain or any other way except to pray. I wouldn't pick fights then leave them for my brother to finish. I'd iron clothes for my mother and polish my father's work boots. I was as penitent as any sinner piling logs on his own sacrificial fire. The bigger the fire, well, the more impressed He'd be. I was exploring my spiritual being to depths I didn't know I had.

I was still inventing promises when Miss Martin called on me.

"Larry, didn't you hear me?"

"Huh? ….no, Miss Martin."

"Stop daydreaming, please, and join us. Spelling, think about spelling. How do you spell snowball?"

The Lord wasn't listening, or, He was listening and not buying it. She did know. Willie was wrong. All those promises were going up in smoke. I was to be sacrificed myself. I was the lamb that the pastor spoke of.

"S N O B A H L E, snowball." I didn't have a prayer—that was becoming too apparent. My first lapse of faith in the Lord…had He heard any of those promises I'd been passing along? Did He bother to keep track of the money I DID put in the collection plate?

"I'm sorry that's incorrect, Larry. Would someone else care to try?" And of course Mary was up to the challenge. It didn't end there....could we spell ...Snowflake? Snowman? Snowplow? Snowshoes? She just kept it going. Snow, snow, snow. Slowly my fascination with the stuff was melting away like Frosty in March...this was unbearable. Was I already in Hell? Oh...if I could take back that dark bitter evening when I cast goodness aside and began my descent down the path of evil and wickedness. On the other hand, why wasn't Eddie Goldberg being subjected to this death by a thousand cuts? By my count, there were at least four other guys slinging snow that night....that night? Was it just last night? So this is how eternity goes on forever... how do I get out of this place? What power do I really have over my fate....oh, dear Lord...I'm stuck!

I glanced at the windows, they had bars, two rows across and three rows of steel vertically. The Reformatory, if I got out of this Hell, I was doomed to spend my life in the Reform School. Miss Martin's once mellifluous voice faded into the raspy whine of a troll-like figure shouting commands, "Straighten that line, you no-good hoodlums!" "Shut your gobs, you pack of urchins!" I heard the crack of a whip and the sting on my back jolted me into reality. It was Mickey. He was poking me with his No. 2 pencil.

"Moose, she's calling on YOU."

"Larry, you're daydreaming again. I'd like you to rejoin the rest of the class, please."

The troll was gone, the bars were gone.

"Frosty the Snowman was a jolly happy soul..." Gene Autry sang from the record player next to her desk.

"Larry, what's number three?" she asked now sounding impatient.

Number three what. I need more than that. Number one I know, or if a guy had to go number two, I knew that. Everyone did.

"Moose, it's on your desk," guided Mickey as though in my thoughts.

On my desk. I looked. A white sheet of paper.

"He was made of snow but the children know how he came to life one day," Gene crooned on.

The Cowboy Code by Gene Autry

1 . 'A Cowboy must never shoot first, hit a smaller man or take unfair advantage.'

I skipped down...

There it was number...

3. 'He must always tell the truth.' I shouted, more than read.

"Thumpetty, thump thump. Look at Frosty go."

I looked to my escape, the windows. Beautiful flakes drifted past obscuring the church steeple.

"Let's run and we'll have some fun now before I melt away." If only Frosty and I could make our getaway over the hills beyond.

"That's all the music we have time for today. I brought a special treat for you all." Miss Martin bent below her desk and brought up a paper bag. "Larry, would you pass out the treats to everyone?"

I shuffled to the front to help. She handed me the bag. I reached in and pulled the treat slowly from the sack. Snowballs. White fluffy coconut covered snowballs. Sealed in plastic, I could smell their sweetness. I gave the first to Mary. She accepted it and put it on her desk then resumed her erect posture with folded hands on the desktop—not the woman of my dreams; someone else's nightmare I guessed. I covered the room passing out the confectionary to each. Then the bell sounded and Miss Martin wished all a happy weekend.

I brought the empty bag back to her desk with the certainty that, like our cat toying with a mouse, she'd pounce on me. She'd been having her fun and now on Friday afternoon, I'd get my due and have the entire weekend to suffer in ruin. Then I'd go to Reform School. I'd expected better of her.

"Didn't you get one?"

"No, Miss Martin, I gave them all out." My jaw hung so slack that I could barely get the words out.

She pulled the desk drawer open, removed an object, and handed it to me. A snowball. Black. No, chocolate. No...black for being bad...black for evil...but with...was that coconut? I was getting the black snowball. Or was it something even more sinister? Was arsenic black? Was that dark chocolate? This must be like getting the short straw to determine who's going to the gallows. My trembling hands wouldn't move to accept it. This would be how it ended, with the black snowball.

"Go ahead, Larry, it's for you. It's delicious."

I'd remembered that being the evil queen's promise when she handed Snow White the cursed apple. Now it was my turn. My mind whirled with fear, indecision, and then a peaceful acceptance of my fate.

....

The huge burning barrel where we warmed our frosty hands in the winter is gone now. So is the merry-go-round and the see-saw. However, the playground is as inviting as it was for my last recess. The first snow of the year falls around me. It falls upon my head, indistinguishable from the white hair. The flakes melt and trickle down my face like the tears of gratitude that crept from my eyes the day Miss Martin forgave me.

Miss Martin isn't with us anymore, although she lives in my memory, in my thoughts, and in these words.

I never told her 'I'm sorry' that day, but I was and still am, perhaps even more so for not having said so ... for not abiding by the Cowboy Code.

"Twenty-eight, Miss Martin, Twenty-eight, that's how many snowballs I had left. That's the answer." I shouted so forcefully that the girls across the street with iPod's in their ears turned to stare, then ran.

"Twenty-eight, Miss Martin...twenty-eight and I am sorry."

A WAY OF LIFE

"For the last time, Larry, get your nose out of that catalog and come here," my mother said as though she'd already decided on a penalty if ignored once more. I hadn't been paying much attention. My face and finger tips were smudged with ink from the Sears catalog. There were still a few days before Christmas – ample time to correct any oversights or bad choices like the Popeye punching bag that didn't last a round or the walkie-talkies that were no different than whispering from room to room except that making them squawk required batteries. My brother and I had been abusing the catalog for weeks. We'd bent so many pages over to mark what we wanted that there were now more pages turned than not, at least in the toy section. We agreed that next year we'd have to invent a new system to avoid confusion. The option of curbing our greed never occurred to us.

I stumbled over to my mother, my nose still pressed to the pages offering metal soldiers and tanks, gas stations with cars, and ranches complete with cattle and horses. She hunched over her sewing machine. "Put that down and try this on. Good Lord, you boys are getting greedy. Look how many pages you've bent over. Christmas isn't about presents…it's about Jesus. It's his birthday!" I dropped the thick book at my feet and put my arms in the air. Now was not the time to be disagreeable or misbehave. There was too much at stake. My mother pulled the white linen gown over my out stretched arms and my head. "Perfect, now put this on your head." She handed me a bundle of cloth.

While it wasn't a towel, it wasn't exactly a hat either. Somehow, she'd taken a bath towel, attached more safety pins than a porcupine has quills, and made it into headwear more suitable for a Las Vegas showgirl.

"There, you look like one of the wise men. You need a staff. Everyone back in those days had a staff." She pushed back her chrome plated chair and went to the hall closet where she rummaged around until she found what she envisioned as my staff – the broom handle. I'd used the same handle the last three years for my Halloween costume. It was the stick to which I attached my handkerchief as the *pièce de résistance* for the hobo outfit.

Unlike Halloween, Christmas wasn't a single day, an evening, it was a season that lasted from the time the first catalog arrived in the mail until the last present was unwrapped, played with then abandoned to the point where by New Year's it looked like an unwanted house guest. The season seemed to get longer each year. My father complained about this. Every year, he claimed, Sears sent the catalog a week earlier. Montgomery Ward took it a step further and sent its catalog out days ahead of Sears. And every year the books got bigger causing my father to wonder how much better his childhood would have been if catalogs of this length had been available to supplement the newspapers in the farmstead outhouse.

As it turned out, however, it was this enormous 'Monkey' Ward catalog that tipped the scales of my mother's patience. Having finished with my nativity wardrobe, she called to my brother, Mike, for his first fitting and measurement taking. Mike was curled up with Katten, the black and white cat, and the Ward's catalog. His red transistor radio rested next to his ear pressed into the fancy embroidered pillow. My mother never raised her voice, at least not until that morning. Mike ignored her calls although her voice stirred Katten to leap from the couch and attack a glittering silver ball hanging midway down the busily decorated Christmas tree. The tree tilted against the window crashing a dozen balls into the glass panes and bouncing on the hardwood floor.

The cat's misstep might have been the proverbial straw that pushed my mother to scream, "That's it, Christmas is cancelled. There will be no gifts this year. No presents!"

She didn't sit still to hear objection or argument, or even for us to make a plea at her feet. She stood, threw Joseph's brown robe on the maple floor and stomped off past my father who'd had the misfortune to amble out of the kitchen with a green spritz cookie shaped like a Christmas tree held in his hand inches from his mouth. With mistletoe over the doorway, he mistook her intentions and opened his arms to welcome her advance. She drove past him so quickly she spun him in circles.

"What did you two do?" My father balanced the cookie in his hand as if weighing the chances he might have to enjoy it in peace.

Mike turned the page of the catalog. He'd missed the entire circus. My father removed the red transistor from his ear and stopped Bing Crosby in mid verse of White Christmas. That got Mike's attention. He dropped the catalog to the floor and sat up stiffly. "I don't know, Larry, what'd you do to get her so upset?" He'd developed an enviable ability to deflect responsibility.

My father put his rough hand on my head which was filling with excuses and explanations all anxious to spill out. "I don't know," was all I could say. I'd have to do better than that old standby which always resulted in a predictable follow-up question.

"Well, you must have done something to bring all of that on..."

I felt his hand squeeze my head as if he knew there was an explanation in there that would be forthcoming if the right amount of pressure was applied.

"Dad, you know how women are," Mike offered a universal male reply that in this instance, resulted in my father's hand being removed from my bushy, black hair. For centuries, men have stood in circles, kicking the dust or sat on bar stools tipping a mug and uttering those six simple words that every human with more testosterone than estrogen understood without further explanation.

I made a note to remember the remark that had a ring of usefulness when there arose a riddle inside an enigma inside a woman. "Yeah, Dad, you know how women are." I practiced the line and it felt good on the tongue.

It must have been pleasant to the ear also, because my father smiled and agreed. It was a magic moment when despite our age and family standing, we could have a meeting of our hormonally linked minds and come to a collective cosmic conclusion. "Sometimes, you just have to give them a hug. Sometimes that's all they want and it solves the problem."

I focused on the bare floor under the pine tree – it was empty – as barren as a vegetarian's hamburger bun. "But, Dad, she's cancelling Christmas, there won't be any presents, no church pageant…no more carols…no more cards or company…no Christmas lutefisk…" It was the possible loss of the lutefisk that seemed to convey the gravity of the matter. Up to that point, I believe he was beginning to see the benefits of a cancelled Christmas. Before my mother's proclamation, the Old Man might have thought there was a law against such a prohibition or he would have called off a few festive holidays himself.

"Yeah, and after almost a whole year of being on our best behavior," added my brother in an absurdly charitable review of our conduct.

The Old Man did a double-take then seemed to think better of taking the time and energy that a comprehensive rebuttal to my brother's exaggeration would require. He rubbed his chin as he considered an answer that would ease the anxiety he must have seen in our faces. "Well, boys, that's another thing you have to understand about women, they always change their minds."

My mother should have been able to change her mind by the following morning. There was after all only two days before Christmas. That was the thought I carried in my hopeful young mind as I raced barefoot down the wooden steps from our bedroom to the hallway and then to the living room stopping at the tree where all of my dreams of toys and treats would be realized. Bare, bare as a monk's cell.

I searched the house for my mother. All I found of her was a terse note that she'd gone across the street to her Aunt Tillie's house to help her get food ready for Christmas Eve.

My mother's absence, and my father's departure to work, afforded my brother and me an opportunity to search the house. We'd perfected our tactics and were as skilled as detectives executing a search warrant looking for the murder weapon. Start at the top, work down, each room worked in a circle, I clockwise and Mike counterclockwise. We began in the spare bedroom taking care to leave no evidence of our intrusion. Nothing, but not unexpected, this was the room she'd used last year and I'd made the mistake of disturbing the wrapping in my enthusiasm to discover the contents. She never cast an accusation, still I felt her stare when I opened that gift, a toy gas station. I knew she was assessing my reaction and I showed an exaggerated expression of glee and surprise. "Too much... you overdid it," my brother later explained.

Neither of us came by this sneaky notion of an early peek at our presents on our own. It was genetic or learned, either way, it came from my mother. It was impossible for her to hold a wrapped gift in her hands without scratching at the tape or giving it a shake. Of course, like all great pleasures, it was the process that enhanced the enjoyment as much as the end result. This one began with considering the wrapped gift from a distance. She was able to eliminate many possibilities with this initial assessment – too big for a toaster, too small for a vacuum. She even worked her keen understanding of present misdirection into the gifts she wrapped for others. A baseball glove would appear under the tree in a box large enough for a bike. A pair of boxing gloves would appear deceptively under the tree in two separate boxes. Once my brother threw out two silver dollars when he didn't consider carefully enough his new Christmas socks—I think he still expects to find them some day if he just keeps checking.

Eying the gift led to lifting, weighing, shaking, and squeezing, sometimes played out over several days. As we grew older and wrapped our gifts to her, we incorporated a variety of countermeasures. A ring would be placed in a small box filled with a few marbles to increase weight and provide some action when shook. Next we would take an old t-shirt and wrap it tightly around the box to provide some texture and confusing bulk. And so the game would go, each year we increased our ingenuity and added immensely to her delight. The gift became anti-climatic which was just as well since by the time we were adolescents she still hadn't exhausted her collection of cheap perfume and had more fake jewelry than most community theaters.

So we came by what some may view as a sly nature through a legitimate family tradition – one that even my normally stoic father joined with some unintended consequences. It pained my father to open the coin purse and while he was a loving and generous man, it was contrary to his nature to buy expensive gifts. Two years earlier, he had found a house dress at Woolworth's, on sale, half-price. He snatched it up, wrapped it up, and placed it under the tree. My mother had done her usual detective work and knew it was a cotton print dress three days before Christmas.

The price tags were always left on the gifts in case they needed to be returned. We typically scribbled over the price on the tag leaving just enough visible for store clerks and for recipients who didn't subscribe to the maxim that it was the thought that counted. In his enthusiasm for a bargain, my father had purchased a size 16, four sizes too large for my mother. Two days after Christmas, my mother walked to Woolworth's, dress in hand to find a suitable replacement. She brought two blouses, a skirt, and some delicates to the front counter to make an even exchange for the price on the dress tag, which listed as $49.95. The Old Man had added the 4 as a joke, a kind of Norwegian satire on his thrifty nature. My mother explained her way out of a fraud charge and when she recovered from the embarrassment, used it as a sterling example why the Swedes should have never given the Norse their independence.

We finished the second floor, moved to the first, then to the basement. We always searched that dank cave last. It was not a hospitable part of the home. I ventured down the creaking planks that passed for steps. I felt the cold damp air hug me like a ghoul in a tomb. The light bulb waited at the bottom of the steps. I waved my hands trying to find the dirty string to pull. It wasn't where it should have been. In my stocking feet, I crept to the cold concrete floor feeling for the next light by the coal bin. The thin string felt as comforting as a life line thrown to a third-class passenger on the Titanic.

Once we mastered the lighting our fears abated and avarice drove us on. Strike two – except for the few boxes of junk that no one had the heart or ambition to haul to the dump and the black bear with the glass eyes and missing canine tooth that used to serve as a rug, all that remained were a few forbidding shadows not worth entering for a gift within my parents' price range. In fact, we'd never found a single gift down below, however when there is the threat of a cancelled Christmas, extreme measures are necessary to find any reason to hope it was all a mistake or a very bad joke and mother rarely made either.

The day before Christmas Eve my trip down the steps from the bedroom was filled with anticipation that the gifts would be under the tree like every other year. Mike, seemingly blessed with deductive powers just short of the great Holmes himself, informed me he had concluded that Mom had simply moved her Christmas headquarters to Aunt Tillie's house. After all he argued, the gift wrap, the scissors, the tape, all normally stored in the hall closet with the Hoover vacuum, were missing.

Mike passed his theory on to my father later that morning.

I studied my father's reaction and detected a hint of panic, an emotion I'd seen only once when he'd reached to pick a ripe tomato from his garden and came back with a rattlesnake attached to his loose shirt sleeve. That was panic, and I saw just a glimpse of that in his eyes.

"I tried talking to her…"

"Did you give her a hug?" I asked.

"Ah, she was in no mood for that. She gave me the lecture you boys should have heard, how Christmas is a celebration of the birth of God's son and it's become a celebration of greed and gluttony. I guess I can't disagree with her…"

"…but what about the presents? And the gift of giving, and it's better to give than receive? That's Christmas too." I fired off my entire arsenal hoping something I said actually made sense to my father.

"I know – the tree bottom is as bare as yours the day you were born. Look, boys, tomorrow is Christmas Eve and the church program, and when we always open the gifts. If there's nothing under the tree by tomorrow morning, I'll take you boys shopping."

I'd never before been shopping with my father. He avoided the stores like Pastor Tuttle avoided walking past Snowball's bar out of concern a parishioner might assume he'd just been tipping one with the fellas. The pastor would toddle a block out of his way to preserve his image. Sometimes, it created quite a maze for the parson, because every block had at least one tavern and going from the parsonage to the Rexall Drug store could result in a three mile hike.

Shopping was limited in Mandan. Greenberg's, our baseball sponsor, for clothes, the hardware store for the things that were of no interest to boys, and F. W. Woolworth, where we could linger for hours ogling each toy, imaging how it could enhance our lives and reputations and dreaming of adding it to our small menagerie of playthings. The dreaming was more pleasurable by ten-fold than the acquisition which was at best unlikely. So it was to Woolworths we first ventured. My father pressed a bill bearing Mr. Lincoln's likeness into our hands, moist with excitement. That would be plenty for the few gifts we needed – one each for our mother and brother. We split at the doorway and unexpectedly met at the perfume counter. My father claimed rights to the Evening in Paris cologne and shooed us away. We separated again and again Mike and I met at the costume jewelry. Mike claimed the rights to a ten carat fake diamond ring and sent me scurrying to what was left, the colorful scarves in the front of the store. My mind raced with the packaging potential of this gift. This year, I'd add a box with loose rice for shaking and spray some perfume on the wrapper for some added sensory deception. Mom would love it and she'd feel even worse for calling off our Christmas.

The gift for my brother was an easy selection. I'd been hearing Mr. Potato Head's siren call for months whenever I had occasion to stroll through the Woolworth aisles. Now, I have to recognize that my mother's judgment concerning our greed was accurate. By my reckoning, Mike would look upon the toy as being a mismatch for his polished tastes and for his age. Consequently, Mr. Potato Head would be abandoned quickly and after a proper time of grieving over my brother's loss, the head would be mine. Lest I assume all the guilt for this, I must add I'd come by this trick via my brother who, by my count, was about five gifts ahead of me through clever gift selection and by having lived for two more years. In fact, I'd guessed he was at that very moment buying a fountain pen that sucked up black ink from a glass bottle. He'd been admiring it since the start of school, somehow fancying that such a pen would create stories Shakespeare would have plagiarized.

We reunited at the drug store where my father had promised root beer floats. I sensed the agony as he dug three quarters from his pocket and placed them one at a time on the counter. Each slap of the coin on the polished wood top triggered an involuntary grimace on the Old Man's chiseled face. We finished the last slurp as my father declared that we'd now be on to Greenberg's for one last purchase.

Our baseball team sponsor's store was where a guy would go if he had a pocket full of paper instead of coin. Mike and I never had occasion to make a purchase at the store although we walked in heads held high knowing we were a part of the team and expecting to be recognized by the lanky Mr. Greenberg himself. In a three piece suit befitting of Mister Monopoly, he approached my father, with hand extended, and a Yuletide grin for the shopping season. An act my father took as the prelude to a rear assault on a wallet that seldom saw the light of day. Mr. Greenberg patted our heads, something we'd outgrown with cloth diapers, and acknowledged our team's outstanding season record, a pretense my father would later explain was an amateur's effort to soften him up. My father recoiled a step and the salesman moved in for a pin, gripping his elbow and dragging him towards the women's dresses. Mike and I settled into the stiff wooden chairs to trade outrageous guesses at what we'd bought each other, each of us carefully avoiding what we'd strongly suspected to be the right answer by giving misleading clues the likes of which would have led me to conclude that Woolworths sold ponies out of the back door.

The wrestling match featuring my father and the slick salesman took longer than regulation, into overtime. At about halftime, I spotted Lucky Joe and ran out to talk to him. He was walking with his brother, the one who had a wooden leg replacing the one he'd lost in the war, and two boys, my age, who he'd introduced as his sister's sons. He was taking them shopping, down to the dime store. The boys, each with long ponytails and impatient faces, tugged at their uncles' sleeves to go. I identified with the urgency, wished them all another Merry Christmas and returned to my brother's side.

At the end of the contest, it was a draw. Mr. Greenberg made the sale and Dad got the floral print dress at a price that the store owner cried would cause him to lock the doors and move to the poor farm. Both wore a winning grin as they marched to the front of the store. "Let's go boys, we've got presents to wrap and you two have to get ready for the church pageant."

Getting ready included a bath that required cleanser and shampoo instead of the usual dip in tepid water and a brush with a bar of the gritty Lava soap favored by my father. And water so hot my skin turned red under the bubbles that floated to my chin offering the opportunity to form a beard the likes of Santa Claus himself sported. Wrapped in two towels and still wearing the white bubble beard, I made a dash up the steps to our bedroom and slipped into the clothes my mother had laid on the bed. There was still no mention of the missing presents, although she seemed more her old cheerful self even singing along with a tinny version of "Silent Night" playing through the kitchen radio. Even though everything she ever sang quavered so far off key that it caused Coffey, the neighbor's Chesapeake retriever, to howl in the summer, I was glad to have a reason to think Christmas was back on.

The bell in the church steeple rang four times which meant we were on time as we ambled through the vestibule carrying our costumes and wrapped gifts, usually mittens or socks, to be laid under the spindly tree and later distributed to the less fortunate as my mother referred to them. I believed they were less fortunate because they got mittens and socks for Christmas. The church basement was alive with excited kids and fussing mothers. The fathers huddled back near the kitchen drinking coffee sharing jokes, smokes, and old war stories. I found my class by listening for Butch's high pitched laughter that sounded like a chicken being plucked alive. The pageant director, a large stern woman of German descent revealed by an accent that bordered on incomprehensible to our young ears, hit on a bit of genius this year. She found the perfect part for Butchie. A role that was unlikely to allow him the freedom to bring the unexpected disasters we'd come to expect from the tow-head little monster as my father referred to him.

Every pageant, the boy outdid himself. The previous year, the mischief maker played a shepherd. Dressed in a long brown robe, he strode forward, toward the manger where Mrs. Berger had put her own living infant in a wooden crib – an arrangement my mother, the Sunday school superintendent, later banned as being unnecessarily realistic. Butchie, the moniker for Melvin that his mother used endearingly and we used mockingly, closed on the infant with the intent to deliver his one line and retreat. It would have been uneventful except someone had furnished Butchie with a staff, presumably to herd his nonexistent sheep. Butchie began his six words and in an expansive move to emphasize those lines, he swung the staff across the stage, snagging Joseph's beard and continuing the wide swing with the fuzzy beard now on the tip into the three candles, representing the completion of the trinity. The cheap beard caught fire and Butchie dropped his staff onto the bales of straw.

In a heroic act, Pastor Tuttle, the church's elderly minister, sprang to his feet, grabbed the water from the baptismal font, rushed to the straw bales and doused the fire. It was Easter before folks stopped talking about that, but my mother clung to the memory and insisted that the pageant director, Mrs. Hildebrand, find a role that would assure no repeats of last year's spectacle. That's how Butchie landed the role as the south end of the north bound donkey. I'm not certain who won the coveted lead role as the student refused to remove the donkey's head.

My recollection of pageants and plays, recitals and rehearsals is that they dragged time out as if someone had laid the hourglass on its side. Consequently, I never retained much of a recollection of detail, just the highlights:

Scene One – three shepherds spy the bright star and declare that observation in a single sentence, delivered in three parts to allow each student a speaking role. Four years ago, several mothers complained that their aspiring actor/actress just stood next to the manger looking stupid. My mother told the women that she couldn't change how they looked but agreed to give each a line. "Hark, there in…" "…the sky, it's…" "a new star."

Scene Two – three wise men, myself included, entered stage right, opposite the lowly shepherds. The tallest wise guy pointed to the yellow star hanging from the church ceiling. "Behold, a star in the East." The next tallest guy came up with a bright idea. "It's as the prophets promised, let us follow the star." The three of us strolled off towards the star.

Scene Three – a battery operated lantern is turned on by Joseph. My mother forbid any form of flame. The small switchman's light illuminated Joseph and the blessed virgin played so splendidly and appropriately by Valerie, the parson's daughter who'd captured my brother's eye last year. My mother observed they were a handsome pair and that such a coupling might move Mike a step closer to the seminary she'd longed for him to attend despite his insistence that he intended to make a career out of throwing a baseball. The blessed couple delivered their lines among two live sheep, a white goat, and the donkey starring Butchie. He'd gotten into the role even swishing his tail in my brother's face. Butchie could be counted on to breathe life into the deadest of scenes.

Scene Four – the three wise men arrive at the manager joining the shepherds and the animals in the little barn, all admiring the holy family. The tall wise man announced, "We, three Kings from Orient Far come bringing…" Now here we were given equal time for each of the kings. I'd moved into the number two slot and was set to continue the royal pronouncement. I pulled my robe sleeve up a bit to reveal the seven or so words I was responsible for. Unfortunately, the scalding bath with soap and scrub brush had faded my crib sheet tattoo. Memorization was the backup and I'd about mastered the verbiage and was about to spew it forth when Butchie swung the donkey's hind end towards me and emitted a nasty hissing fart that made my eyes water and the donkey's tail appear to wither. In an act of self-preservation, I tried to hold my breath to avoid the fetid fumes that seemed to absorb increasing amounts of available oxygen. My stomach began to churn, my lunch was backing into my throat and it required strength previously unknown to me just to stand still until the noxious cloud began to thin. This was no ordinary fart from a child, this was a game-changing contender in the arms-race.

A hard act to follow and whatever I'd recalled of my lines was floating alongside Butchie's gas stirred by the single fan hanging above the congregation. Decades later, I'd watched memory experts with amazing recall of people's names using association. 'That man has large rough hands like a farmer…Mr. Fields.' Without knowing the method, I was saved by Eddie Goldberg seated uncomfortably in the front pew. Gold! "Gold…" I shouted and stalled. Mrs. Hildebrand, in her thick Germanic accent, gave me a whispered hint.

"…Frankenstein and Meryl," I said in my best theatrical voice. It seemed like there should be more so I shouted with glee, "Hallelujah, he's risen, Hallelujah!"

Scenes Five and Six – I just stood there flushed and stunned without any recollection of what occurred although I suspect it concluded with a visit from an angel suspended from the ceiling and announcing "Peace on earth and good will to all men."

"…and may there finally be peace on earth," my mother finished her dinner prayer using about half the time than it took to burn the two long candles illuminating the dinner table. My father added a brief Norwegian

54

prayer in his native language. Then there was a moment of silence sere-naded by the crackling wood fire which my father lit in the fireplace only once each year. Too much heat goes up the chimney.

The seating arrangement was non-negotiable, Uncle Herman at the head of the table, his wife, Cora, sat to his right, then Aunt Tillie, her brother, Bill, then my father at the other end and to his left my mother and completing the family, us boys. The Christmas Eve meal reflected some ethnic compe-tition. For the sole Norwegian and his offspring, lutefisk, kulb, a block of cow's blood mixed in flour and cream, and oysters. For the Swedes, which was everyone else, I guess, mashed potatoes, and Swedish meatballs. Before we passed a platter, my father raised a glass of dark red Mogen David wine and toasted his wife and the ladies who'd prepared the feast. I took the opportunity to steal a glance at the tree, still without a single gift beneath it. I resisted the urge to add a salute of my own to my mother's cooking for fear it would be too transparent as an attempt to remind her about the part of Christmas still missing, but at least we had the gifts we'd bought earlier in the day and the aunts were always good for a silver dollar and some black socks. Those gifts had to be delivered personally and were attached to a kiss leaving a year's worth of red lipstick on my cheeks and the lingering smell of Woolworth's finest perfume, Ode to Joy, in which the older ladies never failed to bath prior to dinner.

The platters had all made the first pass when a meek, barely audible, knock summoned our black dog, Duchess, from under the table and to the front door. I almost beat her there having deluded myself into believing it was the postman making an emergency delivery from Monkey Wards with an entire division of U. S. Army soldiers that I'd circled in the catalog with my mother's red lipstick. It had to be, or maybe the real Army Jeep and the live monkey I'd found advertised in the back of the *Superman* comic, required a special courier. God Bless America, a damn Jeep and a Monkey, ain't America great!

I hardly recognized Lucky Joe, his face, head, and shoulders so covered by fresh snow. And I'd never seen his brother without a beard and with his hair slicked back and a broad smile. The two boys peering between their uncles, I recognized from our morning shopping trip. My mother appeared behind me. There was, in adult parlance, what could only be described as an awkward moment. Lucky Joe seemed to sense this and offered, "Little Moose, he invited us to dinner tonight, Christmas Eve Dinner."

"Of course, yes, sure, please all of you, come in. Dad come here and take their coats."

The four guests came slowly through the old oak door, stomping snow from their feet and followed by a tall dark-skinned woman with hair as black and glossy as a raven. Rhonda was her name and her relationship to the others was left unspoken. She had soft eyes, large and the color of a tanned deer hide. They stood in the living room taking in the foreign smells and shifting uncomfortably. "Dad, you and Bill move the kitchen table into the dining room, I'll get the dishes. *Little Moose*, **YOU,** help me in the kitchen."

Blissfully unaware of the tumult I'd initiated, I followed along with Duchess, who misunderstood our move as a change in venue to get table scraps. In the kitchen, my mother pivoted on me faster than a NBA point guard. "What is this about? You never told me about this. Did you ask your father? Did he know?" She continued firing questions at me. My thoughts moved to formulate a response that would be required as soon as she ran out of steam. A short term solution would have been to blame my father. He was famous for ignoring such information, and had I truly told him, he truly would have forgotten. But by golly it was Christmas, I was under a lot of stress what with memorizing my lines, Butchie farting in my face, and a very conspicuous dearth of Christmas presents.

"I invited Mister Joe and his family when I saw them in front of Green-berg's this morning."

"What were you thinking? What…"

"You're the one who cancelled Christmas. You're the one who said I was greedy and that Christmas is about giving not taking."

I'd never seen my mother stopped in her tracks or speechless. Then the tears came and she bent down and hugged me, lifting me off the checkered linoleum floor and twirled us in circles. My father was right about women, they were unpredictable and they could change their minds faster than a spinning top. She set me down and sprung into action or maybe reaction would better describe how fast she recovered and had the five new guests seated and served, and even blessed with an abbreviated prayer. Lucky Joe found the lutefisk, dried cod fillets brought to near life by a lye bath, and boiled to the consistency of Jell-O to be quite agreeable, even tastier than the netted sturgeon he routinely hauled from the muddy Missouri. The boys stuck to the Swedish menu.

Conversations never lapsed as the ever-urbane Uncle Herman regaled the new ears with tales of his wife's ancestor's voyage on the Mayflower and a story filled with personal details about Teddy Roosevelt's victorious charge up San Juan's Hill. He paused only once to light a cigar which thereafter rested between his fingers but for an occasional puff at a point in a story where a semi-colon might be appropriate. My mother surveyed the scene approvingly, although perhaps aided by Mr. David's wine as evidenced by checks blushed like a Raggedy Anne doll. She opened the dining room curtains affording a delightful view of floating snow the size of cotton balls. There never was a Christmas Eve where time passed so unnoticed or pleasantly. Uncle Herman's cigar was but a mere stub and he slowed in his speech when my father stood, a sure sign that a departure of someone would be eminent.

I hadn't noticed when our guests had arrived that Lucky Joe had carried in a brown paper bag, soggy but intact. He lifted it to his lap and softly announced that they brought a few unworthy gifts for his hosts. His nephews delivered small packages wrapped in yesterday's newspaper to our family members. No one spoke although O Little Town of Bethlehem played on the AM radio in the kitchen and Uncle Herman, head nodded to his chest, gave an occasional snort as a prelude to a symphony of snoring.

I accepted my small package, squeezed it, sniffed at the newspaper, and gave it a shake. It rattled. I wondered if Lucky Joe was savvy to my mother's tricks. I tore into the paper and it revealed Lucky Joe's snake tail, the lucky one with 13 rows of rattles.

Mike had completed his inspection, lift, view, sniff, squeeze, and open. Lucky Joe's foot, the jackrabbit's furry foot that he claimed gave special powers to the owner. A charm Mike would later claim cast a magical spell over Valerie.

My father discovered a cigar packaged in a fine metal tube. He unscrewed the top and breathed in the aroma.

My mother was still assessing her gift, likely the only one she'd not had a sneak preview of in the last three decades. "Oh, good gravy, Joe, you shouldn't have." Her eyes lit with delight when she held a gold cross necklace that sparkled in the candlelight. I'd seen the same at Woolworth's and knew it must have cost the entire Christmas budget.

"Well boys, can you help me with the gifts for our guests?" In an act of generosity that could have caused a coronary for my father who stood and led us to the broom closet where he'd secreted our gifts from the earlier shopping spree. He handed me the gift wrapped Mr. Potato Head and the fountain pen. Mike took my mother's gift which would fit Rhonda and we both watched while my father plucked the bow from her package and attached it to grandma's ivory handled cane which had rested in the closet since her death. He took the silver Zippo lighter with the U. S. Army insignia from his pants pocket, rolled it in some red sparkly gift wrap and set out down the hall.

I believe the only disappointment was when little Lukey opened the fountain pen. I tried to ease the pain by slipping a platoon of green plastic army men into his coat pocket before they departed.

All great meals need to end with a sweet dessert. Every one of our Christmas Eve meals ended with a birthday cake with a single candle. A few years back, Mom explained to me that one thousand nine hundred and fifty-six candles would likely set the house on fire. She brought the chocolate cake with its candle and sang Happy Birthday as she set the pan on the dining room table. Lucky Joe stood and harmonized with her. His brother, Rhonda, the boys, Lukey and Jimmy, joined in the choir as soon we all did. Up until then I'd always viewed the Christmas holidays as a break from school and learning; this was the year my mother taught me that Christmas was not a day in my life, Christmas is a way of life.

OFF THE CROSS

Whack...Whack...Whack... The Old Man swung the dull double-bladed axe at the base of the apple tree. I'd heard him threaten to take down the centerpiece of our back yard every time he spied a neighborhood kid hanging upside down from the highest branches while helping himself to some of the forbidden fruit and when a hefty branch fell in his carrot patch, still, I never expected him to actually chop it down. As with most matters of great import, however, he didn't ask my thoughts on the subject. I sat on the back porch steps and watched. I felt like I was losing one of my best friends. That tree had been my place of refuge, the proverbial high ground since I was tall enough to reach the lowest branch.

Just as the tree fibers began to creak and crack then fall towards the garage roof, Mickey ran from behind the tilting timber quicker than the squirrels darting to avoid the impending collapse of their homes. He was moving with purpose, but he still wore the smile that made him look like a contented orange clad monk.

"The cops, all of them, are at Bernie's. They're all over the station. Put your shoes on, Moose, and come with me." Mickey said these things as though he was making a demand and offering an invitation at the same time.

I stood then cringed as the tree collapsed on the garage roof. The Old Man cursed and threw the axe to the ground. It bounced once, flipped, then stuck in the fresh stump with a precision that would have delighted the Old Man had he intended it to happen. There was a message in all of this about taking a life and then paying a price for it, although it was a message that my youthful mind had little experience with. I didn't want to stay around for what was sure to be a colorful assessment by the Old Man of his newly-contoured garage roof so I pushed half-way through the screen door and grabbed the black Keds. I slipped them on and saw that I was fast losing ground on Mickey who seemed to glide rather than stride. Bernie's Standard Oil Service Station was only three houses down the block. It sat on the corner across from the Foremost Creamery. Mickey was right, as he always was – the cops had the place surrounded. All three city squad cars each with an enormous red bubble on the roof and the three-wheeled police scooter were parked in the lot. Three officers and the chief stood in the back of the station looking at two empty parking spots. They talked and gestured towards the vacant space and then down the alley. Mickey and I eased closer to the barrels of waste oil resting against the back of the white building. The air was full of the smell of petroleum products.

"I wonder what happened here," Mickey said.

"I don't know, maybe someone was killed," I offered insightfully.

"No…it doesn't seem like a murder. Maybe the car fell off the hoist and hit Bernie or maybe they found Lucky Joe died while he was sleeping under the counter again, but I don't think there was a murder. Maybe they're waiting for a murder that hasn't happened yet. Maybe a ghost rose in there…spring is when things come back to life…" Mickey's mind was stunning in its capacity to summon views of reality drawing from a source inaccessible to other human beings.

"Okay, but the whole force is here. It must be something big."

"Maybe they were robbed. It feels like it could have been robbery by crooks" suggested Mickey as though he was homing in on the truth.

"So why are they standing in the back?" I asked.

Before Mickey could put forth a theory, a black Dodge sedan pulled into the alley and came to a quick stop. A tall lanky man wearing a brown overcoat and a white scarf flapping in the wind jumped out of the passenger side. It was Mr. Greenberg. He owned the clothing store and more importantly sponsored our baseball team. He moved rapidly towards the police officer, arms flaying at nothing and spittle flying from his mouth. The chief held his hands up to calm the businessman or at least fend him off before the spit drowned the poor old chief.

"Let's get closer," I suggested.

We moved from the barrels, carefully avoiding the oil spills, to the inner circle, unnoticed. Being small proved to be an advantage in this instance.

"We don't know who stole your car, Mr. Greenberg, but we'll find him, that's for sure," the chief said. "Don't worry, we'll find him." He pulled his duty belt up over his protruding stomach and jiggled it up and down until it settled as naturally as the equator around the earth.

"Like when the Gypsies robbed me blind last summer? How can this happen? You men are supposed to be patrolling at night. That's why we gave you those fancy squad cars with two-way radios."

A tall confident-looking man in dark blue work clothes rounded the corner. It was Bernie, the owner of the gas station and he was frowning…frowning more than when Melon broke Bernie's air hose filling his bike tires.

There was more yelling, more flaying of arms and finger pointing in every direction and at every chest. I caught only pieces of the discussion when Old Paddywacker finally noticed Mickey and me edging closer to the crime scene. "You kids get out of here. This is none of your business. Get." His hand moved slowly toward the black paddywacker hanging with menace on his thick webbed belt. We moved across the alley towards Mr. Johnson's brick home and sat under his carefully manicured pine trees and watched the adults. Lacking the audio, we gained little more information from the confrontation.

"I still don't know what happened here, what do you think, Moose?" Mickey asked with sincerity you were more likely to hear in a good school teacher rather than a kid.

"I don't know," I answered wishing I could do better for someone so genuinely interested in my views. "I thought I heard them say that Mr. Greenberg brought his car in for a repair."

"It was a '56 Chevy, I heard them say that. We have a '51 Chevy and you have a '46 Ford which is good, too. Mr. Greenberg has the '56 Chevrolet with mud flaps."

"Yeah," I answered, once again slightly distracted by Mickey's store of details. "Anyway, he left the keys with Bernie."

"I heard Bernie say they parked the car out back when they'd finished the work and locked the keys inside the station when they closed," Mickey said.

"…and now it's gone. Mr. Greenberg is really mad."

I settled into the manicured lawn to enjoy the show. There was no popcorn for sale so I reached into my jacket pocket and brought out an orange. I pried it into halves and gave a share to Mickey. He began sucking on it while holding it with both hands. It was like watching someone eat in a dream. Then his hands dropped and the orange, peel and all, was gone.

The only evidence of its existence was a faint orange mustache that curled up at the corners of Mickey's mouth.

"I think Toady, the greaser, might have stolen the car," he said at last. "He pumps gas for Bernie at night when no one else is around. He wanted to charge me a nickel to put air in my bike tires. How can air cost anything? That's the kind of person who would steal Mr. Greenberg's '56 Chevy. I bet it was him," Mickey offered. "You still looking for your cat?"

"She didn't come home yesterday not even to eat her supper," I answered without asking how Mickey knew our cat had run away from home again. I also didn't bother asking why we'd shifted into a whole new conversation….there was no explanation for that.

"I saw her last night crossing the street in front of your house. I think it was her. Or, it could have been a cat ghost. Cats have souls you know…."

"Why didn't you catch her?" I demanded without following Mickey into the discussion on cat-souls.

"I was in the car and I wasn't driving. I'll stop when I have my own car. I'll stop for stray cats and for hobos. I wouldn't stop for Toady the greaser, though, now that he's stealing other people's cars. He can drive himself around…"

Large drops of rain drove us away, back to my house where we sought refuge on the front porch swing. This was the fourth day of rain and earlier that morning I'd heard on the kitchen radio that there were more flash flood warnings. That forecast was reinforced when Mom opened the screen door and warned, "You boys stick close to home today. There're storms on the way and you know how fast the streets fill. That young Berger girl got swept away last night, and nearly drowned. There's milk and cookies inside when you're ready." She wiped her hands on her white apron and retreated back into the house, the wooden screen door slamming behind her. She'd been nervous about floods ever since her own father had tipped over in a boat on the Missouri River. Three men lost their lives that day.

Still, drowning, floods and crime could wait, however getting my fill of my mother's chocolate chip cookies couldn't. I ran for the door with Mickey gliding right behind me. My older brother, Mike, was already seated with our neighbor, Willie, at the kitchen table. Chocolate smears on Willie's face told me they'd already had their share and I could only hope that didn't include my share. In front of them were a couple of dozen eggs and bowls of floating color – red, yellow, green, blue, and an orange that resembled the shade of the full moon in the fall. Tomorrow was Easter and today was part of the tradition. In the old days, back when I was a true believer, the Easter Bunny himself would dye the eggs and hide them throughout the house and the yard weather permitting. The family had altered that custom a bit. Now we dyed the eggs and hid them from each other not really caring if they were found again. Last year we missed a few and by the 4th of July the smell was as sharp and thick as the Old Man's comments when he finally tracked them to a hiding place behind the stove. "How in the hell," he asked, "was anyone suppose to find those damned eggs back there?" By the odor, I guessed.

Mickey and I pulled up chairs and with small wire spoons began to sink the eggs into the bowls of dye. At first, we turned out pure reds and bright yellows, but we couldn't resist mixing colors until the last eggs were such a repulsive color we didn't want to risk seeing them again in a potato salad or a sandwich. We took a pre-emptive approach by peeling them for our cat, Katten and arranging them on her abandoned dish in case she came home again. She'd gone missing after the last storm. She didn't much like storms, particularly thunder and lightning. Maybe she'd return when the weather dried out again. She was a peculiar cat with a strange name. I appreciated her eccentricities and unique moniker. She was the star of some of my best stories and with a name like Katten, she sounded like Norwegian royalty to me…Queen Katten from Oslo. It was blissful ignorance until many years later when I asked the Old Man what the very exotic equivalent of Katten would be in English. "Cat," he answered.

"Mr. Greenberg had his car stolen from Bernie's last night," Mickey said when the last egg was put into the wicker basket with the stiff, fake grass. I had been restraining myself from making the announcement because Mickey had discovered the event and it was his news report. He might have mentioned it when we walked in the door, or he might have waited until Thanksgiving. For him, events were not bound by time and I'd long ago given up on trying imagining how things looked in his mind compared to mine.

"Probably those Jonas boys. Two of them already been sent to the reform school," Willie said as he pointed a thumb over his shoulder in the general direction of the reform school. Reformatory school was an odd name because it was neither a place of reform nor a school. It was where they sent boys who crossed the line from mischief to felony. Most of the reforming was done by the kids whose parents threatened to send them there not by the kids actually in the place. My father even picked up the telephone a few times and ordered up the bus to swing by on its next round-up of the town hoodlums. That inspired a reformation even Martin Luther would have admired.

"I don't know who stole Greenberg's car, but I hope old Greenie still has enough money left to sponsor our team this summer," Mike said. He was still wearing last year's green baseball cap with Greenbergs printed on the carefully folded crest that was *de rigueur* for all well-dressed Little Leaguers of the day. G r e e n b e r g s – that was a lot of letters to get on a ball cap.

"Well, he should for all the money I've given him over the years," my mother said entering amidst a great stir at the back door. She was backing into the house facing Sherry and Connie, Willie's sisters. Connie held a small cardboard box between them. Sherry followed. Both girls had been crying and still had tears on their cheeks. "Come to the sink, girls. Put him on the cupboard." We boys quickly abandoned the spectacular Easter egg project and jostled to peer into the box.

Two small ducklings tapped back and forth on the cardboard. One was red and the other, maybe pink. It was hard to tell because either it had been a bad dye job or the little fellow was a natural pinkish blonde. He was also bleeding from the neck, not badly, but he had an obvious gash in the side of his neck which now resembled the bone the old man usually had leftover on his Thanksgiving plate. I reached to poke at it. My mother slapped my hand away. She picked the duckling up and examined his wound. She was a nurse after all and had treated many a wound on humans and on every injured animal or bird the neighbor kids brought to her. It was hard to know for certain how much the chances of a kid or a creature's survival improved upon arriving at our home for our mother's attention. I figured they doubled at a minimum.

"My, oh my, that is a nasty cut. But we'll fix it...what happened?" she asked of Sherry while inspecting the patient she now cradled in her hands.

"Barky bit him. I didn't know he was in the house and Connie and I were letting the ducks run around our room. I caught him but look at the cut Barky gave him."

"Oh, don't worry dear...he'll survive and I'd bet Barky was just trying to play with him." In my view, that was far too charitable of an interpretation of Barky the dog's intentions. He was one of those yippy little mutts that the Old Man claimed could best serve humanity by hanging on a rear-view mirror or a key-chain. Not really a dog, but a toy that pooped on any lawn but his own, made too much noise, and occasionally gnawed on baby ducks.

Our mother reached high into the apothecary section of the cupboard above the flour, lard, and chocolate chips, where she kept her most trusted curatives – hydrogen peroxide, merthiolade, and iodine. Within seconds she'd turned the pink duck a rusty red. The duck scurried on the cardboard and made tiny attempts to quack. It ran in circles when she returned it to the box...much the same as me when she poured iodine into any one of the countless wounds I brought upon myself. Still, to this day, the best medicine I've ever been given was the calm assurance my mother gave me that all would be well and I was relieved when she handed Sherry a tissue along with a promise that the little duck would someday become a high-flying bird as he was meant to be. A virtual ER my mother ran from her kitchen, kids and creatures cured with the wonder drugs of the day: iodine, a smile, and a kind confidence.

The back porch screen door slammed shut. "Old Man Greenberg's car was stolen from Bernie's," a breathless and soaking Melonhead joined the party. He carried a box of peeps in his hand, most of them missing.

"We know, the Jonas boys stole it," Mike offered.

"No they didn't. My brother told me the police hauled the Jonas brothers to the Reform School two days ago," retorted Melon.

"Maybe they escaped already and stole the car," I suggested trying to support my brother's assertion.

"Share your peeps," Willie suggested.

"They can be good for your health," Mickey and I added in unison.

"Oh, that's rich," my mother said with apparent appreciation for our medical insights.

"Have gas, will pass," whispered Mickey to my mother knowing these were the secret words that unlocked gales of laughter.

Melonhead looked at the box regretful that he hadn't eaten them before entering our kitchen. "I have to save the rest. I promised my ma I wouldn't eat them all today." He quickly stuffed the little box into his jacket pocket then pushed it deep.

My father came into the crowded kitchen. "You kids should probably get home. The rain is getting worse and we're going to get some flooding. Your parents likely want you home so they know you're safe." In an instant, they all acted as one and made for the door – a Mandan flash flood was not the stuff of jokes especially if one lived at the bottom of the hills as we did. These were epoch disasters to be taken as seriously as the Frankenstein monster, black mambas and body parts falling off due to leprosy. We couldn't explain any of these things, and even doubted such dark matters existed—until we saw them – or failing that, heard about them from Sherry and Connie who combined to form a wealth of lore on the true mysteries of life.

My brother and I retreated to the screened front porch. In the '50's the porch, front or back, was a simple extension of the house. When there was no television, and one radio and nothing on it except bad news and the latest report on the price of beef on the hoof from Kist Livestock, the porch was the most reliable gathering spot for entertainment. The source of our amusement could be as simple as identifying the make, model, and year of each vehicle passing by on 6th Avenue. Today, however, the show was provided by the rain which came down in slate-grey sheets and soon the water began to flood from the hills above our high-curbed street. There was no more traffic. We rocked on the two-seat swing and sang a song about the old man snoring as the lightning and thunder clapped above.

Out of the corner of my eye, I saw a flash of white streak up the steps and in the open front door. It was Katten and she was carrying something in her mouth. It looked like a large mouse, a very large mouse. Mom would be furious if Katten brought home another mouse as a most reluctant playmate. The last mouse was left in front of the oven door and resulted in Katten being banished from the house for a week and that was a very cold week in November.

Mike had caught the same glimpse and we kicked off the swing to give chase. I saw the point of her tail as she disappeared into the hall closet where Mom kept the spare rugs. Driven as much by our curiosity as our interest in sparing Katten another exile we dashed down the hardwood floor to the closet where we hoped we could intercept the offending rodent. I won this leg of a race between brothers that never ended. I swung the closet door open and there was our black and white cat with her catch. Only it wasn't a mouse, it was a kitten, a solid grey kitten and it squeaked as Katten got it settled into an old brown rug. If cats can smile, she wore one.

Mike and I traded looks of astonishment – a kitten. Last time Katten gave birth, my father did what farm boys did, he dispatched them promptly. Before Mike or I and especially Mom ever saw the little guys. Now we had a kitten. Katten lay down for a moment and the baby nursed.

"See I told you that's what those are for," Mike said satisfied he'd just won an earlier argument about Katten's anatomy. I didn't respond. It seemed more important that we put ourselves to saving the kitten which meant moving it from the purview of the Old Man. Not that he was cruel. He was kind and gentle to us boys. However, he was raised on a farm and as he explained to us, when there were too many cats soon they'd starve. The farmer expected the cats to feed themselves. A place to sleep in return for all the mice they could eat. Least that's what he told us. We heard heavy steps coming up from the basement. Mike pulled Katten and the kitten into his arms. The four of us made for our bedroom on the second floor.

"Put your blanket in the secret closet. She can stay in there."

I did just that. The closet was always a mystery to us. It had a small door that would admit a person the size of a garden gnome and that door, in itself, stirred our imaginations on the matter of what other-world characters passed in and out if it. We could fit inside although saw little point in doing so. There was an empty bottle of liquor on the floor but nothing else, until now when I made a nice nest for the cat and her baby. I shut the door. Soon she was meowing and clawing giving away her hiding place. Mike opened the door and out she flew leaving the new family member curled up and asleep. We gave pursuit with the intent to force her back inside the closet. She scampered downstairs, through the hallway, between the Old Man's legs and out the front door.

"Cat's back," he muttered as we slowed to pass him then flew out the door after the cat. The rain had let up a bit, although the water continued to rush down the street. Mike saw her dive out into the street and paddle across to the storm sewer where she vanished with the flowing water. It was a big entrance. I knew because I'd chased many a ball, baseball, basketball, football, into the sewer. We laid flat on our stomachs in water inches deep and peered into the sewer. On the shelves Katten looked up at us with pride – like a mother with six kittens might. They huddled around her and nursed.

"Go down there and get them," Mike ordered. An older brother can issue such orders and until maybe a guy turns fourteen or fifteen, the commands might as well be on stone tablets. I crawled through the opening although every year it seemed to get smaller. Hanging from the bar which was intended to keep us out, I dropped to the bottom. Probably only a couple of feet but at the time seemed like a drop into Hades. Katten let me take each kitten and hand it to Mike's outstretched hand. He stuffed each one into his partially zippered jacket. After number six made the trip up, I followed. Katten stayed on the ledge until I cleared the bar and made it back onto the wet pavement.

"What now?" I asked. Being junior meant I didn't have to make those difficult decisions.

"We'll put them with the other one," he said like he'd made that decision several times a day.

Getting them past the Old Man was going to be my job. As we hiked back to the house, we decided that I would go around the house, into the back yard, and yell as loud as I could...we would have preferred shooting our guns in the air like the cowboys we admired, but BB guns weren't that noisy. The yelling would work just as well to bring both our parents to the rear while Mike stole back into the front door with six of our new family members.

I took a deep breath and let loose like a Swiss yodeler with a sore throat. It worked...always had and always would. That kid who cried "Wolf" once too often didn't have parents or neighbors like ours. "What's wrong, what is wrong!?" Despite her calm nursing demeanor my mother could panic with the worst of neurotics in two instances: when something was wrong with her kids or when nothing was wrong with anyone. "Are you alright? Look and see, Dad...is he okay? Oh...I knew something was going to happen...things had been going too well..."

"Ah, yeah....he's okay," answered the Old Man as much annoyed as he was relieved. "What are you doing out here, anyway? Good lord, it's always something with you two..."

There was no apparent injury or danger. There wasn't a rabid skunk at my feet, or bumblebees circling my head and I wasn't bleeding. Unfortunately, in the planning phase of the strategy, we didn't allow for a crisis...for some eminent threat and I wasn't able to produce one despite the attention winning performance. With no further plans in mind and no older brother for direction, I just lay down in the wet grass and cried. My mother hugged me, brought me to my feet, and offered any number of reasons I might be scared witless. The Old Man just walked away, likely thinking he was in danger of siring the first sissy in a long Viking ancestry that had endured ocean crossings, life in sod-houses, and two world wars on top of a Depression. I was crying so well, it worried me a little, too.

Mike and I went to bed early that night begging off a bath. I looked like I might break down again and Mom agreed, we were just too excited about Easter and sad about the apple tree's demise, and a good night's sleep that was as powerful a medicine as peroxide and iodine. I fell asleep watching the kittens squeezed next to their mother. She seemed to wear a smile as she put her head down amongst her offspring. Mickey was right, cats do have souls.

With Easter morning came the sunshine and a fresh breeze from across the hills. We marched up the crumbling sidewalk to the First Lutheran Church, the old one with the wooden steeple. I walked stiffly in the suit my brother had handed down to me last year. He was skinny and I was not. In fact, Mom always took me to the 'husky' stack of jeans. I didn't know the meaning of the word, still I didn't like that it set me apart. Oddly, I enjoyed the nickname Moose, but husky—where was "generously proportioned" when I needed it? This year, both of us sported new brimmed hats. Something about kids in brimmed hats just isn't right although many of the church ladies commented how 'cute' we looked. They didn't mean to hurt us, but likely neither did the hornet which stung me when I tried to pet it. Striving to be men, we didn't care to look 'cute.'

The Easter service wasn't bad, not like Christmas where we were dressed like Arabs and given 'parts' to recite. Easter was easy. The pageant had been dispensed with. The old guys who smelled of too much Old Spice, handed out the bulletins, and gave us each a palm branch as we walked in. We were supposed to have waved the branches the week before, during Palm Sunday, but the greenery wasn't delivered until the following Monday. At the appointed time we all shouted 'Hosanna' and waved the branches over our heads making sure we'd pester each other with the leaves until my father gave us a sideways glare. We had no idea what the branch waving was suppose to accomplish, still it seemed to move the otherwise stale air about in the old church. So we went along knowing that within the hour we'd be back home with our Easter baskets stuffed with a trove of candy second only to a sack full of Halloween treats.

This Easter was going just fine. The palms were waved and the plates were passed. Mike and I tossed in the obligatory nickel and, according to Mike's swanky, glow-in-the dark Wyler wristwatch, it looked like we'd be out on time. The choir was on the third chorus of *God Sees the Little Sparrows*

Fall when suddenly a searing cry came from the heavens or the balcony. Butchie had been exploring the ways in which his palm frond could serve as a fan for the back of Mary Kendrick's head. Butch's father, a large awkward man, made a grab for the greenery. Notoriously unathletic himself, Butchie weaved and ducked then tripped and went over the balcony railing. That's the story Mom told us later. I turned just in time to see Butchie hanging with one hand from the oak railing that ran the length of the balcony. He looked like a monkey perfectly at ease with his situation until his mother reached for him; then, without a word or a change in his expression, he let go.

Mr. Greenberg had a tough week what with losing his new car and the rains keeping shoppers from the store. Now to have Butchie land on him was the last straw. He let out a curse that had likely never been uttered from a pew at the First Lutheran Church and one that, by my reckoning, could have broken several Commandments at once—likely a new standard to which my father could now aspire. The cacophony brought the organist to her feet and an uncomfortable silence fell over the congregation. My mother pushed her way over to aid the two fallen parishioners.

Pastor Tuttle likely had a few more words to say on this most holy of days in the Lutheran calendar. We'll never know what epiphanies we missed as the service was abruptly terminated with his brief but sincere wish that God would bless us all. It was my view that God had just blessed us with the most splendid performance I had ever seen under a steeple. When I peeked around my mother at Butchie, the frail tow-headed boy was smiling with the knowledge that he'd outdone himself which, I guess, he had. Kids know good theater when they see it.

Timing is everything. It was still sunny as we strolled home. Without speaking, my brother and I had arrived at the same conclusion. After Butchie's disgraceful if not sinful stunt, we were looking like saints…a status we rarely enjoyed. Now would be the time to break the news of the kittens. The Old Man would be so thankful for our humble and holy presence that he would give Katten and her multitude a pardon. After all it was Easter, and I did glean from the sermon that it was the season for forgiveness and redemption, whatever that meant. I tried not to think about the resurrection part since that seemed to require a death before it could work and I'd seen dead animals before.

Mike laid it out nicely for the Old Man. He had a way with words and sort of weaved it into the whole Easter thing and just like Butchie's scene-stealing performance, it worked. The Old Man didn't say we could keep them but, then, he wouldn't. We were just looking for a reprieve from death and the little guys got it. We could tell from the way my mother looked at him and the way he just shrugged in surrender. We broke away the last half block to tell the cat and her kittens the good news.

It was as grand an Easter dinner as we'd ever had. Mom didn't burn a thing and the Old Man toasted her meal and her beauty with a glass of Mogen David wine. Uncle Herman smashed the potatoes to a smooth perfection. Aunt Tillie commented that the gravy was ready. Uncle Bill, who was deaf, read her lips and wondered out loud whose grave, was ready. The dyed eggs were made into deviled eggs and egg salad. The whites were the shade of my underwear although no one seemed to mind.

The men moved outside to enjoy a cigar and force down sips of a dreadful chokecherry aperitif Uncle Herman brewed once a year using the berries from our back yard. The Old Man told about the cat's adventure and acted like it had always been his intention to provide the kittens with the best home possible. In what turned into a sales-pitch, he concluded his account by asking if anyone knew of someone looking for a brand-new kitten – Katten was the best mouser in town and undoubtedly her offspring would be amongst a rodent's worst enemies as well.

"Mr. Greenberg's car was stolen from Bernie's last night," Mike said apparently feeling old enough to contribute to the conversation, throwing the Old Man completely off his stride.

"Bernie stole old Greenberg's car?" Uncle Bill gave his interpretation.

The Old Man grimaced and blew a large cloud of smoke with such force that he whistled. He liked Mom's uncle although sometimes conversation could be trying. "No, Greenberg's Chevy was at Bernie's for repairs and someone stole it from the back parking lot."

"Greenberg's parking lot? Why would Bernie steal the car, he's got two of his own?"

"I don't know, Bill," replied my father in resigned frustration, "maybe he liked the mud flaps."

"You say he lies like a muskrat? Muskrats don't lie! And Bernie is one of the few honest men in this town! What sort of car was it?" Uncle Bill asked. He kept a pretty sharp eye on things in the neighborhood and likely figured he'd maybe seen the thief.

Mike added what he knew, at least what Mickey and I had told him. "It's a bright green '56 Chevy."

"That's the car Greenberg purchased recently from Midway Chevrolet isn't it?" Uncle Herman asked.

A clap of thunder interrupted the conversation. The rains had returned and we all took shelter under the porch roof.

"Here we go again," my father mumbled through teeth clenching a nearly exhausted cigar butt.

"I know where the green Chevy is," Uncle Bill declared loudly enough to bring his sister, Tillie, to the door to remind him not to shout when he spoke as others did to him.

Dad and Herman seemed to ignore the claim. When it became clear they weren't going to ask and Bill wasn't about to give it up after his reprimand, I asked. A lead such as this demanded at least one follow-up question. I raised on my toes to a height a few inches from Bill's face and I shouted, "Where's the car?" with such gusto that my mother came rushing from the kitchen with the iodine. She was followed by the two aunts, each holding white linen dish towels, likely to use as gauze if the loud shouts were evidence of some serious injury. "Where's the car?" I repeated with even more confidence and articulation.

"Eh? The car? It's in Swanson's garage. I saw that squirt Bobby Swanson drive in there late Friday night when I was out locking up my garage. It's still there. I could see it through the window this morning. I wondered where that no account got such a car." That was the longest I'd ever heard Uncle Bill speak with one breath. He might have used a week's ration of words and half his vocabulary.

"Bobby Swanson? That's Toady! That's who Mickey figured stole it. He's the greaser that pumps gas at night," I added with redoubled appreciation for my friend's insight into the workings of the universe. "Have gas, will pass," I whispered to myself as if to honor those special powers.

"Yeah, that's Toady, all right…that guy wants five cents just to fill a bike tire," Mike offered as further evidence that Bobby Swanson had, indeed, chosen the criminal path we'd been warned against.

Aunt Tillie took Bill aside and communicated with him using a cryptic signing undecipherable to anyone but a World War II code-breaker and the two siblings. We all watched and Dad would occasionally offer suggestions as to the nature and content of the inquisition. Then it was over. Aunt Tillie and Bill joined our small party and she announced, "Greenberg's car is in Bobby Swanson's garage." Evidently, she believed that Bill's pronouncement required further inquiry that only she could adequately conduct.

She said it with such certainty that my father marched into the house and called the Chief of Police, John Sullivan, at home. We could hear him talking through the screen windows and above the occasional thunderclap that still rolled down from the hills.

Dad returned wearing a sour look. "I'm not sure that old bas..." began the old man until he caught my look of anticipation, "...that old bugger believes the story," he concluded.

"It's not that...he's just not venturing out in this storm," Uncle Herman offered. "He hates the rain. On one unhappy occasion he and I got caught in a downpour while we were in the hills hunting Chinese pheasants and other fowl. The man behaved as though he was at Pompei and Vesuvius was spewing forth...unforgivably craven for a man charged with upholding the law..."

"No," responded the Old Man, "he says he has a house full of guests and claims the Mrs. would skin him alive if he left 'cause they're mostly his family. And I don't doubt she would. Besides, he says, Swanson isn't going to move the car in this rain."

"I wouldn't wager my walking stick on that," Herman countered. He tossed his spent cigar out onto the greening grass leaving a trail of hot ashes in the air like a rocket launched towards the Swanson's. He spit out the remnants of the Cuban stogie. "I suggest we get the car back before it disappears again. Summon Greenberg on your telephone and insist that he come bearing arms...his shotgun would do best, I'll warrant." Uncle Herman disappeared into the house down the hall to the bathroom, evidently to avoid an undignified concession to his aging bladder while in pursuit of a suspected car thief. My father looked at my mother. It was her uncle who was directing the mission. And, according to family lore, he'd been at Teddy Roosevelt's side as they charged up the hill in San Juan. It was likely lore that Uncle Herman had authored, still it was the only lore we had. Mom looked at my father then gave her head a slight shake to indicate agreement with great reservations. It was years before I realized that, as kids, we had been learning a whole other language aside from that which was spoken...often we knew it better than the adults who'd unwittingly taught it to us.

Mike and I smelled adventure. A stolen car, a posse—a very old posse – and Mr. Greenberg with a gun. This had the ingredients of a great movie. Except there was no way we were going to be invited to watch it. The women and the posse all repaired into the house.

The three men returned with rubber boots, rain slickers, and umbrellas. I thought the later detracted from the savage nature of the adventure but then saw Dad held our baseball bat under his yellow poncho.

I have to admit, Mike could think on his feet. Out of genius inspired by desperation, he pulled on Dad's coat tail and whispered, "I know where Toady keeps his keys hidden."

"How do you know where Toady keeps his keys? Where are they?"

"It's hard to describe, under the steps, but I could show you. Then, if Toady won't come to the door you can let yourselves in and get the car keys."

Brilliant, simply brilliant the way he pulled that off. Dad didn't say he could come, but he didn't say we couldn't as the three men made their way down the slippery concrete steps into the deluge. Mike took that as tacit permission which gave my father plausible deniability should my mother later confront him with his foolish acts. Least that's how I see it some fifty years later. We threw our shoes off and followed, oblivious to the rain, like street urchins off to view a hanging.

The Swanson place was only across the street then up the gravel alley. That hurt even our toughened feet so we walked on the grass where it was available. We were two houses short of our destination when the black sedan roared past splashing us with water from the puddles. It drew to an abrupt stop behind the Swanson's garage and three men, Mr. Greenberg, Bernie, and a small man carrying a large shotgun got out. To this day, I don't know who the little character was. Except for the gleam of intelligence in his hard stare, he looked like Elmer Fudd in pursuit of the rabbit. The trio wasted no time with plans or warnings and stormed to the garage. Mr. Greenberg pushed the old wooden door so violently it fell from its hinges. There, dry and shiny, was the bright green Chevy.

Bernie looked inside the garage then slid to the back door of Toady's little house. He pounded furiously and shouted for Toady to make an appearance. He added a string of curses that ought not to be repeated in an Easter story. Elmer, the mystery man, shouted for Bernie to step aside as he would blow the door open. Bernie moved with the grace of a cougar and Elmer cut loose with a blast to the knob. It flew open. Bernie, Fudd, Greenberg, the Old Man, Bill, and Herman flooded the house with the precision of the Three Stooges meeting the Marks Brothers. Mike and I wordlessly followed with our mouths agape. We barely slipped in when I heard the faint cry, "Help, Help me."

The posse traded looks then spread out. The kitchen smelled of smoke and burned food. We were about to follow when the Chief and Old Paddywacker pushed past. The Chief shouted, "What in the hell is going on here?"

"Help me. Help me." The plea, now louder and more plaintive came from under the house. The Chief lowered himself to the linoleum floor and put his ear to the cold surface. He screamed for the others to be quiet. "Where are you, Bobby, where are you?"

"In the cistern, I fell through the floor in the bathroom. I'm in the cistern. Get me out."

....

Some five decades later, I stood on the freshly poured sidewalk outside a new picket fence and looked at the fine apple tree adorned with fragrant pink blossoms. I peered at the second story window where my bedroom had been. I closed my eyes and opened my heart. I could hear my gentle mother's words as she sat between our beds that Easter night.

"Redemption is when you get a second chance. It's like when you make a bad decision, but you get to be forgiven for your mistake and get a chance to make it right," she told my brother and me.

"Will Toady get redemption?" Mike asked.

"From what your father told me, he made some decisions that turned out poorly."

"But he said that he just took the car to put it in the garage for the night because Bernie's inside stalls were full of cars that couldn't be moved."

"He said he was going to bring it back the next morning, but he fell into the old cistern," I added.

"I think Bernie will give him a second chance."

"Like Katten, she and her kittens were redeemed, weren't they?" Mike said.

She lay next to our beds in a box stuffed with old towels surrounded by her family. She purred softly.

"Yes, your father certainly gave her a second chance. I'm glad he did."

"How about Barky?" I asked.

"And Butchie?"

"Well, Barky's a dog and he just did what dogs do."

"Butchie's a boy and he was just doing what boys do," I said not knowing why I'd ever come to his defense except to perhaps further the cause for all youthful indiscretions.

Mother took my hand in her soft grasp, "You know how upset you were that Dad cut down the apple tree? My father cut that tree down when I was your age and it grew back. That's redemption, if the tree gets another chance, then I believe Butchie will too. That's what Easter's all about."

TOGETHER – FOREVER

"**Watch out for the snakes, children.** They'll be sunning themselves today, on the rocks." Those were Miss Martin's last words shouted from the steps of the yellow school bus before she turned the class loose for the morning. I paid no heed and loped across the rocks and knee high prairie grass to the Fort Lincoln blockhouses built by the United States military a century earlier. The rough timber structures stood guard over the rolling hills on a landscape bare of tree or bush. Each was intended to be an intimidating presence looking down upon the Mandan Indians who had constructed a village of sturdy earthen lodges amidst the great expanse of trees that lined the mighty Missouri River.

In a rare instance, I was first up both wooden ladders within the nearest fort, pausing only to look through the gun ports which looked suspiciously modern, then up the narrow ladder to the top of the roof – a magnificent view in every direction – a fine location for a fort, unless one was a Indian in the 1800's. I could even see Mandan, home to me and a few thousand other souls. I spotted the railroad depot and knew my house was only two blocks away. Below, the Missouri River, brown and swollen by the melting mountain snows, delineated the traditional boundary between the East and the West, between one civilization and another where the newcomers thought only the savage existed. Mickey followed me onto the catwalk and we used the railing to guide us as we made our way around the rooftop trading speculations about where any invaders would come from, how far we could fire an old musket ball, and whether an arrow could hit us from the coulee hidden by buffalo berry bushes.

"Yikes, here they come!" Mickey poked me in the ribs. "Look – down on the river, they're in bull boats."

I peered beyond Mickey and a hundred years into the past. The river was crowded with buffalo hide boats and big steamers. Black puffs of smoke rhythmically bellowed from their stacks. I heard the hooves of a hundred horses and the cries of cavalry officers passing by. The wind carried the odor of sweet grass over the fort where it mixed with creosol impregnated in the huge timbers and provided an earthy recollection of an ancient redolence. It seemed as though I'd witnessed this grand unfolding before.

I felt a fist thud against my back and fell halfway through the railing before Mickey caught me and stopped my momentum.

"I saved your life, Moose. Arrows were flying right at your fat butt." I looked up and into the bright brown eyes of my 'savior,' Melonhead.

"What are you doing here? Your class isn't on this field trip."

"I volunteered to come along and look after you little goofs." His grin said otherwise. Melonhead possessed few altruistic notions. If he was along, there had to be a hitch. He obviously found a way out of school, or maybe it was the hot dogs that enticed him to "volunteer." A fat wiener could cast a spell over Melonhead—I suspected an unstated kinship between the two.

"How'd you get here?" I hadn't seen him on the bus.

"I got a ride with the pastor's wife, Mrs. Tuttle. Your smartass brother came with us."

"Where's he at?" I asked, hoping for some added protection. I had a strange relationship with Melon. I liked him and admired his innate cunning. And I often learned from him, mostly what not to do, or think, or say. He was an outstanding role model in that regard. However, largely ignored by a golf-addicted father and a life-weary mother, he was less than gifted with social graces and often given to what would certainly be called bullying today. He wasn't the kind of guy you'd ask to sleep over or take care of your pet goldfish for a week, still he was one of the neighborhood kids and had to be accepted with all of his individual faults and foibles like the rest of us.

"Dropped him off in the parking lot down at the Indian mounds. He's with Valerie, the pastor's daughter. They were heading off to the mounds together." He smiled and raised his eyebrows as if there was more to the story, although he'd not be sharing it.

"Let's go down to the mounds." I didn't wait for an answer knowing that he had me cornered like a black-footed ferret with a three-legged prairie dog. He'd toy with me on the fort's rooftop until I became a bore and then we all know what happens to the rodent. I feigned to the left, then cut right, past his clutches and scurried down the ladder, two rungs at a time. Melon, on the other hand, ignored the ladder altogether and plummeted straight

WHERE THE BEST BEGAN

down to the main interior. I heard the heavy thud and quickened my pace. He could move like a mad buffalo with the proper motivation. I was it.

I launched out the door and sprinted across the hill like a rabbit racing for home. It was only to catch my breath that I pulled up at the gateway to the little graveyard – the soldiers' graveyard. I walked carefully into the rustic resting place and sat down on a patch of grass. Small white stones with names, dates, and details carved into them. . . 'William Keen, Private, Drowned 1873.' In the Missouri River, I guessed confidently. I first visited this tiny cemetery with Grampa. He was old and I was young, too young to remember his every word. He told me stories that his father had passed on about the soldiers in General Custer's 7th Calvary. His father had spent five years with the General. That old soldier would bring his son to the cemetery. He said it made him feel closer to his pals in Company C. Grampa told me how hard it was to live at the fort and how the soldiers would swim across the Missouri to desert or to visit the cathouse on the east shore of the great river. William Keen probably died trying to get to Bismarck—something he likely hadn't expected when he woke up on his last morning.

I rolled onto my back, preferring not to sink into a sullen state thinking about death. I dreaded the thought of dying and being dead, and couldn't understand how either was fair. However, being young and alive on that beautiful spring day I guessed that, unlike Private Keen, I had years to come to terms with my eventual demise. A more immediate concern was Melonhead, although he was nowhere to be seen. I lay in the sweet grass and listened to the wind speak of quiet mysteries in a way like no other place else on Earth. The sky was full of clouds. A smiling dog. An eagle. A few in a state of transformation that only required patience and imagination. It was Mickey that pointed out the Indians on horseback chasing the buffalo across the sky. They were all moving fast across the blue and over the river – away from the cities and west towards the Badlands.

"I wonder what they know that we don't," observed my friend of the shapes passing over us.

"Moose, get up, we're going down to the Indian village." Our reverie was broken–Melon had caught up to me and was uncharacteristically charitable in his tone. He offered his hand. Suspiciously, I grasped it expecting to be yanked into next week. I wasn't—he actually helped me to my feet. Was it the allure of hot dogs and potato chips that brought this on? Like a pointer after a quail, he sniffed the wind wafting up the ravine. Given the distance he put between us in a matter of seconds, I picked up my pace to get there while at least some food was left. Like I said, I learned much about human nature from the big boy.

The class mothers, wearing cotton aprons and warm smiles, were waiting at the bottom of the hill in the Indian village where our field trip lunch had been laid out on heavy, wooden picnic tables. It was the same menu every year. Sloppy beans, soggy chips, tepid hot dogs all loaded on a paper plate and surrounded by Orange Jell-O. We washed this down with weak Kool-Aid in Dixie Cups. A mere hundred years earlier, brown skinned youngsters sat where we now devoured the pale sausages buried under catsup and mustard and stretched out in a stiff, dry bun. I asked Mickey if he thought Indian children might have enjoyed hot dogs in their day, or maybe buffalo dogs.

"Indian kids wouldn't have eaten hot dogs and neither would Indian grown-ups. Why would they stick good buffalo meat into a tube? In fact, I'm not sure what we're eating. It's not buffalo and it doesn't taste like chicken. It tastes like a petroleum product…it tastes the same as an empty oil can smells. I eat them on account of the good texture." As usual, his answers left me with more questions, but I couldn't formulate the words. I changed the subject, "What popsicle flavor do you think still needs to be invented?"

"We should have the rainbow Popsicle next; it would have something for everyone. That should be the next flavor they invent. I've wondered before what a rainbow would taste like."

Other people looked at a rainbow and imagined a pot of gold at one end. Mickey saw it as an opportunity for everyone to get a bit of something. I had no words equal to this gem either, but being a teacher, Miss Martin did. She tapped a spoon against a Kool-Aid pitcher then announced that we had a busy afternoon ahead, complete with lectures on the culture of the Mandan Indians and a bus trip to a site south of town where we would be awed and inspired by a collection of old bones that scientists were digging from the river banks. From her point of view, it would be a shame to waste a day running unfettered in the hills without expanding our appreciation for the wonders of science and formal research methods. After lunch, we were to gather at the parking lot and resume our trip. Mickey and I used the hot dog bun that always remained after badly planned wiener consumption to quickly mop up the bean-sauce, mustard, and Jell-O blend left on our plates then slipped away to track down my brother and Valerie. They had skipped lunch and would miss the bone bus if we didn't find them.

It was Mickey that heard them giggling inside the Indian mound where the entrance was barred with tree limbs crossed like a jail cell door to keep out trespassers. A sign warned all who thought to enter that an archeological dig was underway and violators would be punished, probably hung from one of the readily available cottonwoods or maybe from the sun dance poles in the mounds where once bone needles were pierced through human skin and then attached to the pole by deer hide strips. These earthen mounds, made of timber and soil, were once home to the Indian people who first settled in this haven hundreds of years earlier. Grass thrived on the mounds and the roots held the dirt in place as surely as cement. You could probably squeeze forty people or a dozen buffalo into the circular mound. It was Mickey who crawled through the rough bars and encouraged me to follow. I also could hear my brother's distinct giggle, the one that involuntarily launched out his chest when he was about mischief. My brother's giggle was similar to what I imagined would be the laughter emitted by the Joker before he sprung another diabolical trap on the citizens of Gotham City—or maybe Scrooge foreclosing on a mortgage before his epiphany. Poor Valerie!

Beyond the entrance was a womb-like darkness. We shuffled slowly into the dank interior with me hanging on to the tail of Mickey's t-shirt which bore substantial evidence that he had recently finished a picnic lunch. Between the two of us, we probably had enough leftovers spilled on our shirts to provide us with supper. I could feel the cool earthen walls with my free hand as we moved deeper into what had been a family's lodge. I could smell the odor of a thousand fires which burned in the center of the structure. I could still hear the giggles, although now it seemed they came from outside the thick walls, on the backside, and then they faded away.

I tugged at the shirt-tail, "Let's go back, they aren't in …"

When I fell, my grip on his shirt was so tight that I pulled Mickey with me down into the abyss. Somehow though, he executed a mid-fall maneuver that allowed him to hit first and cushion my face-down landing. Feeling the thud that forced the air out of my chest was my last memory until a gentle hand on my forehead brought me back to my senses.

"Mickey, is that you? What happened to us?" I asked without having the breath to convey the alarm I felt.

"Remember the warning sign, Moose? We found out why it's there. We're in an archeology hole. It must be where they're looking for dinosaur bones and arrowheads. No wonder we never find any if you have to go down this deep. Remember, we were walking into this mound. We couldn't see and you wanted to leave. Now we're down here."

"I think I might have broken in half if you hadn't landed first. Are you okay, Mickey?"

"Sure, I'm fine. I'm glad I landed first if it helped you. You've been resting—sleeping, maybe. We've been down here for a while now, but I think you'll be okay. I've been watching you for signs." Mickey had stayed by my side. I wasn't surprised by his patience and loyalty, although when I paused to think about it, it almost made me cry. I didn't know how I could ever repay my friend. I didn't even know what he'd want to be paid with.

As I peered straight up into the darkness of the archeological dig, I thought I could see a star shining through the smoke opening of the mound top far above our predicament.

"Just take a deep breath and relax…you're trying too hard to make your head clear; it knows how to take care of you."

I took a deep breath to let my head follow Mickey's orders and immediately felt a bit better until I realized how afraid I should be. Here we were, lost in the bottom of a pit – no sounds, no people, but just enough light that I could discern Mickey in the blackness. Overall, it was an assessment that made my stomach turn and sent a chill through me that I hadn't experienced since last summer while watching the wranglers turn the baby bulls into steers. Unexpectedly, the name William Keen rose in my mind and I wondered if he had had time to feel as frightened as me when his life changed in an instant. Then I felt my hand being squeezed and the apprehension eased. Did Private Keen have someone close enough to reach out a hand during the young man's descent into a deep dark vastness? We sat and as my eyes continued to adjust to the dark, I saw a peaceful smile in Mickey's eyes. It was a look that I would today expect to see in the countenance of a Tibetan monk deep in meditation. With that recognition, the words whispered like the cemetery wind through my mind: "And all will be well; and all will be well." Had William Keen also been comforted by these assurances? Maybe in my case, all would be well. Maybe, as usual, Mickey was right. The class would form at the parking lot and Miss Martin would take roll. When our names were called and we were missed, a search would be launched. In fact, they were likely searching for us this very moment and within minutes Miss Martin would be hugging me with the delight of finding a lost puppy. That thought would carry me through, like waiting for the rapture beside the banks of the Jordan River, knowing you're one of the chosen.

Unfortunately, our confidence was constructed on a premise that was permissible only in a hypothetical equation because we lacked a single piece of information that wouldn't be available to us until the next day: Melonhead, in an exceedingly brilliant display of stupidity, had answered 'here' for me during a roll call taken by Miss Martin when our class gathered after lunch and before the grand bus tour. And as luck would have it, that obsessive tattletale, Mary Beth, wasn't near enough to Melonhead to note the offense and tell on my porky friend. The dissection of any tragedy almost always produces evidence of multiple failures. Ours began with crossing the trespassing signs, followed by Melonhead's prank, and then two more repetitions of the stunt when roll call was taken at two additional stops. My father was working a double shift at the Northern Pacific Railroad. My mother was caring for her ailing Aunt Tillie. My brother, normally a trustworthy soul, was blinded by the pursuit of his lust for the preacher's daughter, Valerie. And Mickey's parents ... well, I'll just say Mickey was a free spirit who was never restrained by parental bonds.

Even those poor souls waiting naked for the rapture by the banks of the Jordan, come to the realization that the time has passed and it's best to get dressed and get going. When it dawned on me that Miss Martin's warm embrace might not be in my immediate future, I asked Mickey, "Are you scared?"

"Of what?"

"Of anything – of everything, the dark…"

"Dark just means there's some light missing, but you can still find it. The light is always there for us."

"Okay, forget the dark, are you scared of bad guys coming in here with a sack full of rattlesnakes and throwing them down here with us?"

"Why would they do that?"

"Because they're bad guys! You've seen just as many Westerns as me…bad guys do that stuff, that's why! Aren't you scared of anything?"

"Like what?"

It could be maddening trying to pin Mickey down, although at the same time, it was illuminating in a way I could feel but couldn't express. "What if nobody ever finds us? Shouldn't we be screaming for help right now?"

"I don't think there's anyone to hear us, but you can scream if you want…it might just make you lonelier, though. Crying and screaming can sometimes make you feel more alone. I tried it once. It was pretty noisy and wet, too. The main thing to remember is that we're not really ever by ourselves."

"Why?"

"Why what?"

"We're alone down here by ourselves! Why aren't you afraid of never being found?"

"I'm not afraid of never being found and I don't feel alone because I'm still connected."

"Connected? Connected like you have important friends or relatives that are coming to rescue us?" I recalled the Old Man talking about how Harvey, the owner of the creamery, was connected to the mayor who was connected to the governor who granted special favors to the creamery.

"Yes. And no. I'm connected and so are you. When you're connected, you can't be afraid of being by yourself…"

Just as I edged near some comfort from Mickey's voice, coyotes, a pack of them, opened choir practice on the prairie. "Ahhh! You hear that? Yeah, you're right, we're not alone, and we're connected to something else to be afraid of— those coyotes. A whole family of them—they can probably already smell us. I can smell us. They could come tearing in here and eat everything but my shoes." I couldn't imagine that even the most ravenous beast would deign to devour my worn-down Keds with the cardboard inserts where once there were soles."

"They might smell us. And they could probably see us, but I don't think they want to be down here in this pit any more than you do unless they're coyotes that like gnawing dinosaur bones. Besides, if they did jump down here and eat you and me, then we would just return to where we came from before."

"Mickey, are you nuts?! What do you mean? You mean we'd go back to…to…to what? To where?"

"We'd just go back to the place that's always been there. To your home before you had this one."

"Geez, what are you talking about? Are you talking about heaven and God?"

"That's what some people call it and Him. That's what we were taught to call it and Him. It's where everything is all of the time and you're a part of it—right now."

"I don't feel a part of anything right now and I don't think there's another kid in the world feeling this lonely and scared."

"Well, you know, God could be afraid and lonely. And connected and brave all at once."

"He could?!"

"Sure...with Him, all things are possible. At least, He'd know what it feels like."

"Could He be happy and sad at the same time?"

"God is both all of the time. And he laughs a lot and dances, too. He even farts. He invented farting."

"God doesn't fart...that's a sin to say so!"

"It's just hot air...God made hot and air and He can make them go together...there isn't any commandment that says, 'Thou shall not let one.'"

"Maybe that's how Melon was created. God was doing the polka, he farted and Melonhead was born." I managed an exaggerated chuckle which actually made me feel the slightest bit more hopeful.

"You shouldn't be too hard on Melonhead. He acts like he's brave and tough, but he's probably the most scared and lonely kid of all. I think his parents probably like him, they just don't like spending much time with him after all those other kids they have. What sort of parent would name their kid Melonhead anyway? And don't forget, Melonhead is Melonhead. You're Moose. Who would you rather be?"

"I don't think Melonhead is his real name, but I don't want to be him either way. I think I want to be me. I guess I like being me. I've never wanted to be anyone else."

"Boy, if your mother could hear you now that would make her happy. And God, too. He and your mom would be happy to hear that one of their creations worked out okay. What do you like most about being you?"

"Well, I try to be good most of the time. I don't swear hardly ever and I never stole anything except my brother's underwear, but I put 'em back in his dresser when I was done with them. And I'm nice to animals and old people. I'd rather not be so "husky" on the outside, but I think I mostly like being who I am inside."

"The inside part is the most important part. That's where you spend most of your time. I think that's mainly why people are afraid of dying. They like being who they are and they think they'll die inside and outside and it makes them sad to think about it."

"But if they're dead, aren't they dead on both sides."

"Remember that run-over squirrel we saw? It was dead on the outside, but what had been on the inside was still alive. That's the part in you and me and squirrels that is the little piece of God inside of everything that's alive … that's the real you…that's the you that you like. It's in your heart that God writes all of the secrets of the world."

I put my index finger to my lips. "Shhhh! My mother told me that the indent on my lips was made by an angel. She said that when I was born, I had all of the knowledge of the world, but an angel came and pressed her index finger to my lips and said, 'Shhhh!' I wasn't supposed to tell what I knew so the angel sealed my lips…"

"You should never forget about it when you get older."

"You mean if I get older…you sure seem to know a lot for a guy who snores in Sunday School. Right now, I'm still scared and my chest hurts and I'm getting really cold and I'm still in this pit…"

"Well, if you're a so worried about that why don't you just walk out of here?"

I looked around just in case I'd missed a ladder or a rope, an avenue of escape. "What? There's a way out of here?"

"Sure, I found it while you were resting…" And with that he grasped my hand, stood, and guided me to what felt like a plank inclined upward. We followed the wooden bridge up toward the rear of the mound where excavated dirt was being piled then began to feel our way toward where we imagined the entrance was. Still very mindful of our earlier descent, I closed my eyes, tight, and followed Mickey's lead with my hand back on his shirt-tail. When my Keds hit empty space, I opened my clenched eyes and we were again at the entrance. Mickey had already slipped through the wood bars and I followed breathing deeply the cool night air and freedom.

As one, we fell to the ground then sat up and looked around for signs anyone had even been here earlier in the day. "Hey! Anyone here? It's us. We're here!" It was a question more than a declaration. We waited, heard nothing but the distant baying of coyotes, and lay back on the damp earthen mounds. We weren't found, still we weren't lost any longer either. I mumbled a word of thanks to Mickey and to the heavens which were filled with stars and a rising full moon. "There never was anything to be afraid of," my mystical friend offered.

"Yeah, maybe, but…I still don't get that connection stuff…what are you connected to?"

Mickey sat up and surveyed his body. "Nothing." He held his arms high and wiggled them to prove no strings were attached.

"But in the mound you said you were connected and that's why you have no fear."

"I am connected. We're connected… to the moon, to the stars, to those spirits hopping around the Sun Dance Pole."

"I see the stars and the moon but…"

"Close your eyes again, then you can see them. You can feel them. You're connected to them and all living things, past and present. You were made that way by God, the Creator, and that little part inside of you is still connected to all of it."

A fresh breeze from the Missouri River bottoms carried the voices of two hoot owls calling each other. I thought for an instant about how the Indians must have felt down here in the darkness when the forts inhabited by soldiers loomed above them. I squeezed my eyelids closed, perhaps the extra strain would invoke the dancers' image. I didn't see the Indians dance and didn't hear the beat of the drum. I did hear Mickey's breathing and that provided a semblance of connectivity.

"I don't see them or hear them," I pronounced after less time than it would have taken to tear off a Milky Way wrapper.

"Yes, you do–you just aren't letting yourself. Try again and this time don't think about candy bars."

I did and I did, or at least it seemed so. There was the presence of others before us. I neither saw them nor heard them, still they were there and I was connected to them as sure as they were attached to the Sun Dance Pole by long rawhide strips. The young dark men leaned back away from the Pole that represented the Creator. There were others, on horses, paints and sorrels, riding through the camp in the moonlight. And there was...

"Little Moose, why are you here with my people?"

Now I heard them! Now I was reaching them and they even knew my name.

And I could feel them, one of them shook my shoulder. "Little Moose..."

I opened my eyes, still feeling the magic, feeling the connection. Lucky Joe shook me again. "Are you having a vision Little Moose? Why are you here? Did you see my great-grandfather? He was performing the Sun Dance." Lucky Joe squatted next to me.

The connection I had been feeling was so much more alive than reality that I was having trouble trying to sort out the two. "I was feeling the dancers...I was with them...and we were with the Creator...God."

"I know, I come here when the moon is full and share that with my ancestors."

"Mickey says we are all connected to each other, to the stars, the sun, the moon, to everything."

"Mickey is very wise. Creator made it that way."

"We were left behind and fell into..." I bawled out the entire story and felt my fears being relived and relieved with each detail. Lucky Joe listened patiently without interruption as adults are seldom inclined to do. In the pale moonlight, his profile was like the man on the back of a buffalo nickel, except he had a baseball cap, a Mandan Braves cap, instead of feathers and a single ponytail pulled tightly to the back of his head.

"It's a lucky thing your friend here took the fall for you. Now, we need to get you home."

He'd taken half a dozen steps in that direction before my short legs moved and then I had to hurry to catch up to him and Mickey at his side.

We followed a worn trail along the river. Except for the occasional slap of the beaver's tail or a leaping pike falling back into the dark waters, the night was silent but alive.

Lucky Joe slowed as we reached an area where the river banks crumbled beneath our steps. My thoughts moved to fear of falling into the swirling waters or worse, the quicksand. Even Tarzan knew enough to maintain a healthy respect for quicksand. "Are you ever afraid, Mister Joe?"

"Of what?" Both my companions shared a complexity of conversation that required patience and more importantly the necessity of engaging as many brain cells as there were stars.

"Of anything? Of quicksand, drowning, freezing to death, or maybe someday being caught by cannonballs and having your head shrunk?"

"No. And those cannonballs won't shrink your head. Might remove it, but it's cannibals that do the shrinking and they don't live in our land. And I doubt as many of them existed as white people think...probably a few of them deserved a head shrinking."

I knew that "no" would be his answer before it even rolled from his lips. Of course, I had to ask, "Why?" and hoped he wouldn't respond with "Why what?"

"When I was about your age, my grandfather took me for a long ride into the hills, on pintos, little Indian ponies. We talked about many things. He explained the great Creator. He told me how I was connected to the Creator and to everything the Creator had made. Then grandfather disappeared."

"He died? Did God take him?" We'd been studying about the rapture in Sunday school and that event was still on my growing list of fears despite the lesson Mickey had just delivered. Seems adults are determined to make certain each child, by the time of puberty, has a full basket of fears to drag around the rest of their days on earth.

"No, he was beside me then he wasn't..."

"Were you afraid?"

"I was young, it was growing late, and I wasn't sure how to get home. Yes, I was afraid."

"What did you do?"

"I talked to my pony. I told her we needed to go home. She turned and headed towards where the sun would be setting in a few hours. Me and the pony were one spirit. It gave me great comfort...the pony seemed pleased, too."

"Did you get home?"

"As the sun was setting, Grandfather returned. He asked how I knew the way home. I told him the pony just carried me back. He asked if I was afraid."

"What did you say?"

"I said that I was very afraid."

"So you are afraid of being alone?"

"No, because I am never alone, the Creator was with me, grandfather told me that, and His pony was with me." Lucky Joe let it be at that when we came to a fallen cottonwood tree blocking our path. The roots of the enormous tree reached out to the river bank. The top of the leviathan had fallen into an abyss of thorny buck brush and brambles. Lucky Joe seized a branch and pulled himself up. He extended his rough hand and pulled me up. Mickey had already scrambled over the top and waited on the other side. We took a breather at the top. And as if he'd never paused in his story, "...and I could see my grandfather riding up ahead of me, especially on the hilltops."

"So he never really left you?"

"No, he did, or he thought he had. Grandfather had very poor eyesight in his later years. He couldn't see me, but my young eyes saw him. He believed he was out of sight. I never told him any different."

We trudged along the rough trail littered with rocks and tree roots grabbing our ankles, veering away from the river and reaching a summit from which the lights of Mandan were a welcomed sight. Mickey and Lucky Joe were right, the fears were pointless. Why should I be afraid of having my head shrunk or the world coming to a blazing conclusion? I was wasting my time and dampening my joy with fears. We struck out again, towards the highway, and a flashing neon light.

"So were you never afraid again?" I felt like I was gaining some ground understanding what my friends were telling me.

"Once, I remember being very afraid, although it was cowardly of me. I'm not proud of that time. It won't happen again."

That comment begged an inquiry. "What happened?"

Lucky Joe didn't answer but increased his stride down the hillside towards the sign I could now read that proclaimed, 'Liquor up front, poker in the rear.' I needed all my facilities on maintaining what, for me, had turned into a sprint which required attention to each badger hole and coyote den dug into the steep slope.

"There's a phone inside, you need to call home." Lucky Joe opened the rusty metal door and held it for Mickey and me to enter. The place smelled of beer, smoke, cow manure, and perfume. Three men and a blonde woman, each wearing cowboy hats, and strumming guitars blasted their melody from the back of the bar. A dozen couples danced around the small square wood floor in front of the band. Lucky Joe pointed to the rear where the black pay phone was mounted on a wall covered with auction posters. He reached into his pocket and dug out a buffalo nickel pressing it into my hand. He told me he'd wait outside. I'd never used a pay phone and told him so. I still remember the look on his face, not fear, but of trepidation.

We walked past the long bar, reaching the halfway point, when a short man with big callused hands twirled on his bar stool and grabbed Lucky Joe by the shirt collar. "Whoa, whoa hold on there, Shit' n' Bull. Strayed kinda far off the happy huntin' grounds, haven't ya? How about I kick your skinny red ass all the way back to Custer's last stand?" The man parked his black hat on the bar and seemed ready to enforce his threats. It was like the classic barroom face off I'd seen a hundred times at the movies although a whole lot meaner and uglier in real life. I stepped back a pace or two hoping to see Lucky Joe drop the offender with a roundhouse or fill him with lead, although I'd never seen Lucky Joe with a six shooter. It was a nastiness without any kind of thrill or entertainment—nothing you'd want to watch while eating popcorn and sucking syrupy theater soda.

Instead, my friend, followed by Mickey, merely walked through the man. Now 'walking through' doesn't do justice to what I witnessed nor was it grounded in what is generally accepted as reality. I lack the words to adequately describe the event. My friend was nose to nose with the man whose face resembled a bulldog, and then Lucky Joe and Mickey were behind the man moving to the pay phone. Bulldog wore an expression as if a pair of rabbits had just slipped through his legs and he lacked the mental capacity or soberness to act on that observation. He just stood there, beer glass in hand, and jowls trembling.

I backed over to my friends and Lucky Joe already had my brother on the telephone explaining our plight and assuring him of our good welfare. Since Mike couldn't drive, my mother was still nursing her aunt, and the Old Man had stopped at Snowballs after work, we agreed that walking would be an acceptable option, actually the only option and not all that arduous given that we were within a couple of miles. I welcomed the hike. I had to discover how Lucky Joe had performed his magic. It had been an entire day of miracles, magic and illusions and I was having trouble figuring which was what.

Without a glance back at the bar or its patrons, we walked out the rear door and made tracks into the road ditch. Lucky Joe refused to travel the highway at night. "Too many drunk men." The newly sprung grass made for easy walking in the ditch; the only danger was slipping on the beer bottles. There were questions racing through my mind about our fall, about the bar, about the universe, but they still hadn't formed into the single query I thought Lucky Joe might answer. I knew I'd think of it tomorrow, but couldn't wait, so I just went for simplicity.

"Were you afraid of that man in the bar?" Not exactly a Perry Mason-like question, still I had a plan, a tack.

"What man?"

The wind fell still and my sails collapsed. "The man at the bar who called you rotten names and said he would kick your...your rear end on account of Custer's last stand." I suddenly felt tears in my eyes and a choking in my throat.

"Little Moose, sometimes what you see is not there. Sometimes, the Creator puts things in your way to test you – to teach you."

"There was no man?"

"Not everyone you see or think you see is really there..."

"But I saw..."

"Use your mind, use your senses, all of them, not just your eyes. Your eyes can lie, just like my grandfather's eyes misled him into thinking he was out of sight. Sometimes there are problems put in our paths like giant cottonwood trees to step over or go around. What would happen if you didn't believe you could get past the cottonwood?"

"I'd be lying cold in the woods, crying."

"Cross the street before that milk truck gets closer."

The three of us raced across Main Street and into Bernie's. I still had two dimes and dropped them into the Coke machine. Lucky Joe removed two bottles and we shared, sitting on the curb next to the coiled air hose. Cars pulled into the station, over the air hose activating the bell and parked at the pumps. Toady, wash rag stuffed in his rear pocket, dragged himself from pump to pump, car to car.

"You said you were ashamed because you once were afraid…"

"You'll pester me the rest of my life if I don't tell you. My grandfather taught me not to be afraid. He showed me how I would always have the Creator next to me, even in death, especially in death. He taught me how to use my senses to connect to the Creator's power over everything. I learned how I was connected to the trees, the animals, and to my people. Then I let Grandfather down."

We both took a shot from the Coke bottles. I shared mine with Mickey after carefully wiping the bottle lip with my sleeve. The moon, full and splendid, cast our shadows on Bernie's white walls. The air smelled of gasoline and other petroleum products. I'd learned to wait for Lucky Joe. He valued his words and didn't cast them about without thinking. That took time.

"During the war, I was in an airplane, flying over China. Two Jap Zeros shot our engines out. The plane caught fire. I made for the door, opened it, and was going to jump. I froze at the door. I was scared Little Moose, I couldn't make my legs jump. I wouldn't let go of the sides of the door. I let my grandfather down. There was nothing to be afraid of. I was jumping into the Creator's arms…"

"I'd be scared shitless…" I'd heard the Old Man use this phrase and never used it, although now seemed like the right time. Lucky Joe shot me a look of disapproval. He never cursed, least not in front of women or youngsters. "Did you jump?"

"There were two more crewmembers behind me, Leroy and Bobby. Leroy pried my hands from the door side and Bobby kicked me out. I must have pulled the rip cord because my chute opened and I landed."

"Is that why they call you Lucky?"

"When I met up with the two fellows who'd jumped ahead of me, they said, 'Joe, you were so lucky, that plane blew up just after you jumped.'"

Beads of sweat formed on my friend's forehead and it seemed a tear rolled down his cheek.

"Well, you were lucky..."

"Not so for Leroy and Bobby. Because I froze in the door, they didn't get out in time and died. That's what fear does."

I was far too young to offer words that would have mattered. I stood and walked towards home, mostly ashamed that I'd pressed Lucky Joe for an answer. Mickey walked by my side until Mr. Johnson's house then as was common for him, vanished without speaking. I felt a hand on my shoulder and heard Lucky Joe, "Little Moose, do you think your mother has some of your Aunt Tillie's sugar donuts? I haven't eaten today." I assured him that I knew where they were stashed and would get him a bag when we got to my house.

True to my word, I slipped through the back door, into the kitchen, and returned with a dozen greasy donuts in a brown paper bag. We sat on the wooden steps and shared.

"Could I walk through Melonhead the way you went through the bulldog in the bar?"

"Do you suppose I could have a glass of milk?"

I returned to the kitchen and grabbed two glasses and a quart from the refrigerator. The house was dark. The front porch swing squeaked and through the window panes I saw two figures, just their heads, inches apart, moving back and forth. I could hear Mike's giggle and surmised Valerie was the second head.

Lucky Joe was down to the last three donuts. I offered to get more but he declined.

"If it's fear that is keeping you from going through Melonhead, then you can."

"Go through Melonhead?"

"Go through fear, Little Moose..."

Mr. Joe finished the last two donuts and the quart of milk without another word and then slipped quietly into the shadows of the night and of what had been the day.

I imagine that my class had a truly outstanding learning experience during the afternoon that I missed. I imagine they saw some remarkable bones. Whatever it was they did and whatever they saw, I understood now that we were all in it **together – forever**.

JAZZ

Miss Martin had surrendered the notion of pounding any more learning into our distracted minds. It was spring and the last day of school, the kissing cousin holiday of Independence Day. In the rear of the classroom, Alvin, Simon, and Theodore sang in their best Chipmunk voices. Mickey, at his desk behind me, joined in the chorus. He actually sounded like a chipmunk although he looked more like a very contented monkey. Next to the RCA phonograph, the girls wearing frilly print dresses, giggled and fussed with setting out the homemade cupcakes and cookies. With a pink ribbon in her hair, Cathy P. stirred a bowl of grape Kool-Aid with a large silver spoon.

My eyes were fixed on my favorite part of the classroom, the paned windows that stood ten feet high and ran the length of the wall. From my seat next to the portals to the world, I'd seen the leaves turn red, yellow, and orange and then fall to the ground. Frost and fluffy flakes of snow hugging the branches came and went. The first buds held my attention for hours and the light green leaves were back heralding the end of the school year. A robin, who had built a snug nest now full of eggs, sang from a nearby branch and watched Mr. Barnyard, Senior, push the rotary mower beneath the tree. The whirling blades made a rhythmic clicking as the janitor clipped the grass one last time for this school year. The windows were tipped open at the bottom and allowed the sweet aroma of fresh cut lawn to sweep past.

We'd be freed early on the last day, at noon, and a single task remained before the treats were served. Each desk had to be cleaned including scraping any gum that might have found a home on the bottom. Two Piggly Wiggly paper bags set on the tiled floor next to my legs, one bag for the garbage and the second to bring home the items of value. After an hour of cleaning, only a baseball was destined for home. I'd found it in the back of the metal desk where it had rolled after the last game in September.

The other bag was filling with broken No. 2 pencils, chewed erasers, and crumpled sheets of papers, some containing my best work of the year, clearly marked on top with a large red C or D. Then there were the other papers and they were the ones that had my stomach in knots. I'd gone an entire school year without a concern, but then last night, as my brother, Mike, and I lay between the sheets of our new bunk beds, he tossed me a curve ball or maybe a slider. He told me about three boys in his class who weren't going to be promoted due to bad grades. I'd always thought that was another hollow adult threat like when the parish priest told Melonhead that he'd go blind. I know he could still spot a pocket full of sunflower seeds or an undivided Root Beer Popsicle from a half a block away. But now, it seemed they were serious. I know Miss Martin had told my mother that I was unmotivated and a daydreamer. The Old Man translated that into 'lazy', a tag I wouldn't deny when it came to school work. Lazy was one thing but being flunked was a rep that could stay with a guy forever. 'He flunked fourth grade', they'd still be telling that story when you're in the nursing home. As the casket was being lowered, the pastor would remind the mourners, "Larry flunked fourth grade. I pray he can make that right with the Lord."

I returned to my cleaning chores. There was a brown knit glove. I could have used that on the day the temperature dipped below zero. I'd just kept my left hand in the coat pocket until I was able to pilfer a black leather glove lined with rabbit fur from my brother and finish out the winter with mismatched gloves. A green cateye marble, the only one not lost in the May Day Marble Tournament. While the Russians were parading their missiles in Red Square, we were battling for keeps in the big circle in the playground. Every May 9th, fortunes were made and lost in the sand.

A headless Peep from my Easter stash was near the ink well. I took a bite. It was like biting into petrified Styrofoam. I remember stuffing the little chick into my sweater cuff during a spelling test. I'd chewed the head off, then Miss Martin had appeared over my shoulder. I think she thought I'd a crib sheet up my sleeve. I dumped it smoothly into the desk well where it remained until today. It went into the keeper bag. My dog would have it as a treat tonight.

Without much enthusiasm, I dug back into the pile of papers. I pulled out *What I did on my Summer Vacation*, an annual favorite of mine and a topic I had much to say. It earned me a B-. If I could have kept with that theme throughout the year, I wouldn't have a worry. I tossed it into the keeper pile on the chance I'd need to plead my case later. The next paper was *The Pilgrims and the Thanksgiving Turkey*. It had no grade. I'd forgotten to turn it in. I twisted in my seat to show Mickey, but he was in a trance singing with the Chipmunks and paid no attention. Jumping to my feet, I ran with paper in hand to Miss Martin's desk. She was putting the finishing touches on the report cards with a red pen the size of a carrot. Maybe it wasn't too late.

"Miss Martin, I found my Thanksgiving paper. Can I turn it in?" I could hardly find my voice.

"May I turn it in?" I was in 12th grade before I realized why teachers always answered a question with a question. She reached across the desk, as did her exotic perfume, and accepted the proffered masterpiece. I did know a thing or two about Thanksgiving Turkeys, specializing in legs, and felt confident that I'd at least snare a C. She read just a few lines then handed the paper back. "I'm sorry, it's too late for you." She returned to marking cards without even looking me in the eye, like when the jury walks back into the courtroom with a guilty verdict. They always look away from the man they're about to hang.

I'd played my last card and it didn't make a full house. 'Too late for you.' Was that what they told the flunkees? 'It's too late for you.' I suspect those same words were used when the inmates made their last walk down Death Row.

I resumed picking through the mess. A guy's desk took on a life of its own as the school year passed by. On the first day, you flip open the clean wooden top and there it is, empty and smelling of cleaning solvent. It's so exciting to put the freshly sharpened pencils in the tray, along with a couple of erasers and a virgin box of crayons. By the end of May, I couldn't even close the top and it had taken on an unpleasant odor. I'd even noticed the last two weeks that Miss Martin's nose twitched like a rabbit as she walked by.

I'd got to know my desk from top to bottom, even the underbelly. Every month, a bell would ring and Miss Martin would shout out a warning for every student to seek the shelter of his or her desk. There we'd sit or lay waiting for the nuclear bombs to strike. I'd felt pretty safe under that substantial wood and steel. Safe until we'd gone to see the "House on the Haunted Hill." Before the movie, a newsreel showed an A-Bomb exploding in a mock town. It became clear to me that under the desk was just a good place to be atomized.

More papers, this time, I pushed them right into the trash bag without any assessment. The time had passed for self-reflection or remorse. I was working down towards the bottom. It was like dissecting a living thing. My hand felt something foreign when I dug in, a sandwich, deviled ham, with a single bite about the size of my mouth in the middle. I remembered that Cathy P. had given it to me. I'd tried it and didn't like it. Rather than embarrass her, I'd just slipped it into my desk. Now it was green and fuzzy and smelled like when the toilet backed up. Into the trash bag, the dog won't even enjoy this, except to roll in.

I checked on the whereabouts of Miss Martin then lifted the pencil tray revealing my stash of spitballs rolled and ready. The spit ball launchers, stout red rubber bands and paper straws lay mixed in. I scooped the little arsenals into my hand and quickly tossed the incriminating evidence into the trash bag. A shame I'd never had the chance to fire across the aisle at Tommy or Jimmy. I imagined, across the Pacific Ocean and several thousand miles away, Russian Generals shared the same sentiment.

I'd forgotten all about the shed rattlesnake skin and rattle, thirteen rows of rattle. Mickey and I had scared Cathy R. so bad with the rattle, she'd wet herself. She'd been just sitting on a playground swing when I snuck up behind her and shook the rattle. A shout of 'SNAKE' was all it took to paralyze her with fear. That little incident earned me a big red U for Unsatisfactory in the comportment department of that quarter's report card. Miss Martin had counseled my mother that perhaps I was immature. The Old Man just said I was a *Dumme Skitt* to do that. Immature, *Dumme Skitt*, what's the difference? The skin and rattle joined the baseball and the peep in the keeper's bag.

Alvin and the boys stopped singing and Miss Martin clapped her hands to get our attention. "Class, you may take a break and get into a single file line at the sink. After you've washed your hands you may get one cupcake, one cookie, and a paper cup of Kool-Aid." I sprang from my chair but still was only third in line. Despite the notations in my report card about a lack of motivation, in matters such as the cupcake line, I always strove to be first. The girls stood behind the cloth covered table and monitored us boys to make certain we'd not exceed the allotment of treats. Cathy R. stuck her tongue out as I passed her cupcakes. I'd apologized already as part of my penance, although she seemed to be holding a grudge. I think it was the embarrassment of the wet undies. In my defense, that wasn't something I could have foreseen.

Mickey and I took the treats back to our desks. I could hardly choke down the chocolate cake, my stomach felt like I'd swallowed a concrete block. Too many memories were rolling over my mood like an approaching thunderstorm. I laid my woes at Mickey's feet. He flashed that chimp-like smile and quoted that noted philosopher, Doris Day. Mickey simply said, "*Que Será, Será.*" They, Doris and Mickey, were right, whatever will be, will be. I could clearly see the logic to that. I finished the cupcake with renewed gusto and made a final push to finish the cleaning. If I had to come back next year, I wanted to start with a clean desk.

The last three issues of *Superman* comic books went into the keeper bag. During our visits to the library, I'd made it a point to check out big picture books. They were well-suited for reading the comics during the twenty minutes Miss Martin had charged us with getting smarter through disciplined reading. Hidden inside the last *Superman* issue was the answers to a pop quiz. Tommy had given them to me. He'd copied them from a crumpled piece of paper in the waste basket next to the mimeograph machine. List the presidents in order of their dates of service was the question. Tommy hadn't known the question just the answer and well, there was a reason the purloined paper was in the basket. It had the order wrong. Miss Martin had interrogated us after the quiz. How could we both have exactly the same wrong answers she wondered? I suggested that it was because we were equally stupid. That got a note home to my parents. The Old Man laughed and agreed with my assessment.

A signed photograph of Roy Rogers went into the keeper's bag. I'd separated it from the letter welcoming me to the Roy Roger Riders Club. It began, '*Howdy Partners,*' and then laid out the rules for the club. Even a cursory review of the rules revealed some personal failing that likely would have resulted in my expulsion. *Rule One: Be neat and clean.* I seldom was. Now if that rule had pertained only to Sunday morning, until church was over, I could have upheld that regulation. After that, it was hopeless. I'd seen Roy wrestle guys in black hats to the desert floor, fall off mountain cliffs, and rescue Dale Evans from a runaway horse-drawn wagon and still 'Be neat and clean.' Then there was *Rule Six: Study hard and learn all you can.* I wouldn't be on the verge of flunking had I been a disciple of Rule Six. In fact, of the ten rules, I abided by only one, *Rule Eight: Eat all your food and never waste any.* It was clear to me that the welcome letter and the small membership card were best suited for the trash bag. While I have my short comings, I refuse to be a hypocrite.

Other than the lint and unidentified crumbs, I was down to the last piece of paper. It was from the church Christmas play, my lines to be given at the pageant where the kings and shepherds showed up at the stables. I was a king that year but should have made an appearance as a butcher because that's was I did to my lines. I'd misplaced the script with my only speaking part. I'd asked Mickey what to say as we came on stage. He whispered in my ear what he could remember from the last pageant which happened to be on Easter. So, dressed in my finest royal robe, I trundled onto the scene to join the blessed virgin next to the manager and proclaim for all to hear, "Hallelujah, He's risen, Hallelujah."

I was still pondering my brief moment on stage when the bell rang. The last bell of the year. It spelled freedom as sure as the Liberty Bell rang in the tower in Philadelphia. I patted my desk top like a cowboy pats his horse's neck after a long ride down the trail and thanked her for the year of faithful service. After one last glance out the window, I picked up my two bags and shuffled to the back of the classroom. I left the Piggly Wiggly bag with the deviled ham sandwich next to the metal trash can and took the last place in the line of students. Miss Martin stood at the doorway, kindly wishing each student a farewell and handing them the last report card of the year. On each card a single X would determine your future. Two boxes were available, Promoted or Retained. The power of the X. 'Too late for you' echoed in my head and with each step grew louder.

I felt a light tap on my shoulder as the line stretching toward my doom grew shorter. It was Mickey with a smile in his eyes. "*Que Será, Será,*" he whispered. "*Que Será, Será,*" "*Que Será, Será.*" Doris Day's lovely voice sang in my head. "*Que Será, Será.*" Then it was my turn.

Miss Martin smiled and stooped to give me a hug and a pat on the head. I looked at her pretty face and her mouth covered with a hint of red lipstick was moving. I didn't hear her. She could be offering her condolences and saying she looked forward to having me in her class again next year. She'd say that just to comfort me. I looked down at my feet then to her hand, smooth and delicate, it held the small card. There were C's and D's in lines of perfect penmanship and then 1's, 2's, and 3's for comportment. I accepted my fate and trudged out the door. "Turn it over," Mickey said as he followed me to freedom or damnation. "Turn the card over."

An exaggerated X in red ink spilled over the box. "Promoted!!!!" I'd passed!!!! I wasn't on the road to perdition or the reform school. Once again, the Last Day of School was a glorious holiday, a celebration of liberation, an exuberance known only to poor students and freed slaves. I skipped down the hall ignoring Junior's admonishments not to run. Don't run, did he think Papillon walked away from his prison on Devil's Island? I was a freeman on my way to the ball fields.

I was the last to arrive and the first to be picked after Willie won the crowning grip on the baseball bat. He'd pitch and I was his catcher. Everyone got a spot on the team, the youngest selected last. The oldest player ran the game and acted as umpire. A guy worked his way up and everyone respected the natural system.

The score was shouted out loud at the end of every inning and disputes were settled by recounting the progress of each batter. Other than that, the game proceeded without much structure and free of adult intervention. Maybe that's why baseball is America's game. At the sandlot level, it's a geometrically perfect, free-flowing game with a place for all to play regardless of height, width, or age.

The First Lutheran Church bell sounded six times from the nearby steeple. The game abruptly came to a close. Not because of any time limitations, score or completed innings, but it was supper time and that trumped most anything including baseball. I grabbed my dusty catcher's glove and the Piggly Wiggly bag and loped towards home with the lightness of a colt turned out to summer pasture. Not a care in the world. No homework. No responsibilities. Like the Gypsies, I'd often admired from afar.

A delicious bouquet of aromas filled the air as I passed through the neighborhood. The Zimmers, they were having pork roast and sauerkraut. The McDonald's would be enjoying corned beef and cabbage. And as best my nose could tell, the Olsens were frying up liver smothered in onions. I rushed past their house and on to my own where I was certain I'd find chicken and maybe fried potatoes waiting on my plate.

The old screen door slammed behind me as I tore into the kitchen coming to a sliding stop on the black and white linoleum floor at my mother's feet. I handed her the most important document since the Declaration of Independence, my report card. "Oh, good gravy, Larry, you got an F in Arithmetic."

"No, turn it over. I passed. I'm promoted." She obviously didn't empathize with my fear of flunking. I stood tall, ready to accept the praise as she turned the card over and noted the big red X.

"Sit up now, it's time to eat and you have the piano recital at seven-thirty."

The recital—in my anxieties of the morning, I'd forgotten about my début on stage. I'd promised to come home right after school and practice my piece. I joined my brother and the Old Man at the table. He was studying my grades. He dropped the card next to his plate of boiled chicken and fried potatoes. He made no comment but did shake his head from side to side before spearing another Russet off the serving plate. Mom said her usual grace which she could string out longer than the Gettysburg Address. I silently added a special request for success at the recital and thanks for the help on the report card.

I could hardly choke down the old rooster Uncle Bill had provided for the table. There was a good reason my mother had boiled it until the skin hung like rags from the bones. It was a tough and tasteless old bird, but it was the new knot in my stomach that killed my appetite. Like all great performers, I was not immune to stage fright. I kept my eyes on the floor. I knew my brother was gloating from across the table. It was me who'd agreed to take piano lessons in return for a transistor radio for my birthday. Greed always has a price. The lessons began right after Christmas. It was winter and music wouldn't interfere with baseball, or swimming, or just screwing off which is how I'd intended to spend my summer days. Now, only the recital stood in the way of my autonomy and my plans.

When excused from the table, I sprinted at an Olympian's pace up the creaking wooden steps to our bedroom and my closet. I dropped my clothes on the floor and kicked them under the bed where I could find them the next morning. In the closet, I tore my black pants from a hanger and slipped them on over my lucky underpants, the ones I wore when I was promoted to the fourth grade. I snatched a short sleeved white shirt last worn Sunday. I pulled the black Oxfords out of the box they'd lived in for the last four years. They'd been my brother's and then passed to me, box and all. The Old Man kept them looking new with his best Army spit shine. With the aid of a silver shoe horn, I eased my stocking feet into the tight shoes. I took a couple of steps. They squeaked a little and hurt a lot.

I grabbed the hand-me-down tweed blazer which had been on my side of the closet for over a year. In a natural flow of the right of primogeniture, many of my first-born brother's clothes migrated from the north side of the closet to the south side. The clip-on tie fell from the pocket and onto the floor. I snatched it up and clipped it to my unbuttoned shirt collar. I'd talked Mom into the clip-on after the Old Man had pulled my traditional tie so tight, I passed out at church in the middle of the reading of the Gospel. I headed towards the steps, pausing at my brother's dresser to add some Butch Wax to my hair, just enough to spike the bangs into my formal hairstyle. I tossed the jacket over my shoulder and zipped down the steps taking the last four with a single jump. I was ready.

My parents and brother were waiting at the front door. The Old Man checking his watch, "Put your coat on and let's go. We're late."

I slid my left arm through the sleeve and reached back to add the right arm. I couldn't reach it. Ever the helpful brother, Mike, slipped behind me and wrenched my right arm behind my back just as he'd seen Verne Gagne do to Dick the Bruiser and into the sleeve. It had been for the Christmas Pageant that I'd last donned the coat. Evidently, I'd grown since then because I couldn't get my right arm through the sleeve. This wasn't going to work as my recital piece required both hands.

"Oh, good gravy, Dad look at that, he can't get the jacket on..."

"You feed him too much."

"Oh, I do not! He's just built like my brother – husky."

A man of action, the Old Man twirled my brother around like a top and right out of his blue blazer. "Here wear this." He tossed the coat into my arms and flew out the door followed by my mother who was still protesting the insinuations that she was responsible for my growth. Mike gave me a shove out the door and at the same time yanked the tweed coat from my back, a remarkable feat. I rushed down the concrete steps pulling the blue coat on. It too was a little snug, a handicap for a piano player who needed the freedom to sway with the music. The bottom of the coat almost reached my knees, although once I was seated on the piano bench no one was likely to notice. I once recalled seeing Liberace wearing a full length mink trimmed coat. I tried to button the blazer but couldn't reach the holes. No matter, all great pianists wore unbuttoned jackets on the bench. I was ready.

The Old Man was taking long strides and put a ½ block distance between us before the first intersection after the library where I spent so many pleasant evenings reading about the world. I ran to catch up and did so before they'd reached the American Legion. I began to skip, careful not to step on any cracks. It was a glorious May evening, a slight breeze filled with the smells of spring's new unfolding. Birds sang their twilight songs as we arrived at the front entrance. It was a gleaming white building intended to resemble something built in ancient Rome which is no easy task when building with concrete blocks instead of marble. I marched in with music in hand. The Legion smelled of booze, cigarette smoke, and fried foods, a wonderful blend for the senses. Out of habit, the Old Man started up the steps to the bar. My mother caught his coat tails and tugged him back. "Dad, it's downstairs. You can stop up there after the concert."

We followed the Schmitt family down the steps and into the hall. There on stage was the instrument of my performance, a black grand piano. Surely, my recital piece, *The Indian Snake Dance,* would thrill the assembled audience on this grand instrument. It was a far cry from the 800 pound upright painted with Benjamin Moore 'Sunset Beach' tint of satin oil that I pounded on daily. If it had ever been in tune, it certainly had that shaken out during the 200 mile trip to our house in Uncle Kermit's cattle trailer. The Old Man set new standards for cursing when he and his brother pulled that whopping pile of wood, wire, and ivory into the 'music room.'

As I strolled down the aisle lined with tan metal chairs occupied by families, friends, and neighbors, I could imagine a standing ovation after the *Snake Dance.* I closed my eyes and could see a call for an encore and the youngsters in the audience dancing Indian style around my piano. I practiced a couple of modest bows as I approached the stage. I thought I heard an elderly woman saying, "There he is," as if catching a glimpse of a celebrity. I mounted the wooden steps moving my fingers nimbly to warm them up for the task.

The number three chair. That's where Mrs. Davenport pointed when I arrived by her side. She'd made a solid tactical choice, like number three batter in the lineup, the guys who could swing the big wood. The Babe, Willie Mays, Ted Williams were all in the three hole. I strolled over and nestled between two girls, both of whom had painted their lips red and eyelids blue. It was good I sat between them to offset the makeup. The room was filled with voices and moving metal chairs, everyone trying to get a look at their favorite player. I heard Mrs. Davenport say that #6 and #8 were backstage throwing up. "Scratch six and eight," she said to her assistant who was also her husband, a pinched faced man with a perpetual scowl. He pointed to me. "You, move down to the number nine chair, quickly."

The clean-up hitter. I could see that strategy working. Save the best for last. I moved to the end seat just as the concert began. My brother sat in the aisle seat of the fifth row and sought to entertain me. He'd seen some local hoods giving the finger. He had about a half dozen versions of what that gesture meant, all furnished by Melonhead, normally a fairly reliable source of street culture. Like a ball player on the bench trying to distract his opponent, Mike set about surreptitiously giving me the finger. Scratching his eye with his middle finger. Rubbing his head with his middle finger. Sitting on all but his middle finger. In defense, I closed my eyes but was still drawn back to discover what new imaginative technique he'd invented. The last gesture, his middle finger in his ear, brought a sharp reproof via the Old Man's gruff whisper.

My attention focused again on the concert, number three on the bench, Charlotte Berger, a homely girl dressed in red gingham, a gingham dress, gingham socks, and a gingham bow in each pigtail. *Clair de Lune* was her piece. Quickly replaced by Betsy Debois wearing white from head to toe. She pounded out *Piano Sonata No. 14 in C-Sharp Minor*. Things slowed as Gloria Lee dragged her leg covered with a heavy plaster cast to the keyboard. Even without both feet, she thrilled the audience with *Ah! Vous Dirai-Je, Maman*. Not a home run but a stand up triple.

I can't recall the rest of the players because I tuned them out and put myself into what decades later came to be known as "The Zone." I envisioned the *Indian Snake Dance*. I played each note in my mind's ear. My fingers moved as each note danced in my head. Apparently, I was a little too deep into the zone because new #8 poked me and pointed to the piano.

I rose from the hard metal chair and marched towards the piano. The music was scrunched into my hand like the papers the Old Man filled the wastebasket with at tax time. I pulled back the heavy bench and sat on the embroidered pillow. Just like Liberace, my jacket tail hung over the back of the bench. I'd loosened my collar at about the #7 player and the clip-tie hung cockeyed off to the left of my gig line. As Mrs. Davenport had instructed me, I sat up straight and reached to place my music on the piano rack. My brother's jacket strained at the seams. The fabric made a twisting agonizing sound as I tried to lift my arms to the rack. Finally, I made it but something tore. I heard the rip.

I resumed my perfect posture. Looking out over the audience, I knew I had them eating out of my hand and I'd yet to play a note. I announced my piece with the seriousness of a pastor at the grave site. **The Indian Snake Dance**. I slowly placed my hands above the ivories pausing just for a moment before I stroked the first key C followed by a D then an E and then for 17 measures it flowed as did my sheet music blasted away by the enormous stage fan. My music had taken wing. I lurched forward to snatch the music, but the jacket restricted my movement like a straight jacket on a mad hatter. Then it was gone with the wind. Not to worry, Mrs. Davenport had stressed to each student the importance of memorizing the piece. Of course, I hadn't. However, I knew the notes repeated the same pattern. My right hand kept that pattern going. I threw my head back like Ray Charles and twisted my torso swaying with the music. I glanced at the audience. They were swaying in The Zone with me. The notes, the music just flowed from my heart, from my soul and down my fingertips. The liberty of the creativity of playing never felt so good. Music never sounded so alive.

I kept it flowing, until I felt the sharp claws of Mrs. Davenport's right hand digging into my shoulder.

....

It's been decades since my recital. I'd moved on to a summer of baseball, swimming, and enjoying fanciful trips around the world during the long hours in the library . I hadn't thought of it until last night when I spent a lazy evening in a Cajun joint in the French Quarter. A hot sweaty evening for the five silver haired musicians pouring their sweet melodies into the night. The waitress, in a skirt not fit for the Baptist Church, opened the window behind the piano player. Unflustered, he kept the music flowing as his few sheets of music took wing landing at my table and bringing with it a revelation. I'd discovered JAZZ that night back in Mandan. Oh, I wasn't the first to play the unfettered notes, but in my little world I had liberated notes from the confines of staffs and flats and notations—I had discovered the sound of freedom. And with that discovery I also learned that sometimes it's best to play from the heart than by the rules.

"Thanks anyway, Mrs. Davenport."

Ridin' Tall

"Don't your family ever throw away anything useful?" my weathered friend wrinkled his nose at the brown paper bag of garbage I routinely delivered to the beat-up metal cans behind our garage. The chore only paid 50 cents a week, nevertheless, that would have bought four candy bars and a ticket into a Saturday matinee at the Mandan Theater.

"Your mother is a very generous lady; your father is a tightfisted man. I never find anything in what you leave here. I may not come back if this situation doesn't improve." Lucky Joe was handicapped with a war injury, still he easily managed the proud bearing typical of Mandan Indians as he turned and began to stride down the rocky alleyway to the next can. Long braided black hair bounced on his back.

"You're not gonna find anything better there, Mister Joe... the dogs tipped it all yesterday," I reported. "But maybe you could wait here a minute."

"I have a schedule, you know," Lucky Joe replied. I'd already veered in the direction of our modest two-story prairie home and set out at a pace only a youngster inspired by a good idea can maintain.

Lucky Joe had moved down to the Johnson's twin cans while I was gone. Certainly, there might have been better pickings there ....old Anton Johnson was an engineer driving the passenger train down the line, a good paying job in the fifties. He tied his cans down to the painted wooden rack so the dogs couldn't do much more than give a perfunctory sniff then lift a hind leg on the rack as a gesture of ill-will toward the parsimonious Johnson.

I was back before Lucky Joe had moved on to Ohm's Café. I caught up and pulled on his tattered shirt tail.

"Here, Mister Joe. My Aunt Tillie made these." I pushed a handful of tinfoil towards the old man who appeared hesitant to accept my offering. "They're donuts rolled in sugar."

"Ah....well, your aunt is a very generous woman, too, but I find little of use in your cans," offered Lucky Joe as thanks.

"Yeah, I sorta know what you mean." I held up my right foot and showed off one of my ankle-high sneakers. "See the holes? You can see the bottom of my foot. Dad said I had to wait till school starts to get a new pair. That's two months away. I'm supposed to stick cardboard in there for now, but it keeps falling out."

I thought I detected a faint smile on Lucky Joe's face before he observed, "I saw you at the dump yesterday."

"That's cuz my dad brought some of the aunties' garbage out in the trailer."

"I know, I went through it after you left. Nothing that I could use."

"I'm going to be in the parade tomorrow. My whole team is marching."

"Gene Autry is going to be leading that parade. On his horse..." shared Lucky Joe. Was he joking?

"Ah, really? Gene Autry is coming to Mandan? I don't know – why would he come here?"

"'Cause I asked him. He was in Montana and wired me that he would be passing through. I asked him to ride in the parade and the rodeo. Yesterday, he wired back that he'd changed his schedule and would be in town today." With that, Lucky Joe swirled like a bobcat dodging a boat-tailed bullet and sauntered away munching on a golden brown donut. I watched him meander up the steep hill past the café and towards the railroad viaduct where the hobos hung out.

A shove to my back sent me to my knees on the rocks sticking through the sparse gravel surface. A laugh followed me to the ground. Only one kid, Melonhead, could emit such a diabolical sound using only a great store of wind and a very large mouth. I'd been looking everywhere for Mickey, but got Melon – a theme that would enlarge itself in a variety of manifestations as my life unfolded. I pulled myself up, dusted a couple of sharp pebbles from my knee and turned to face my older neighbor. He wore his usual jack-o-lantern grin. He held a two foot long single stalk of rhubarb in his big freckled paw. Like the donuts, it too was coated with sugar.

"Rhubarb's ready." Melonhead cracked off a big piece in his mouth. That grin held even as he chewed.

"Wow! Where'd you get that?"

"Old Man Johnson's...through the fence."

I gave a low whistle. "He'll shoot you if he sees you in his back yard." I recalled how Willie had taken a BB to the butt the day he slipped inside the high white fence to retrieve our baseball. The ball would have gone into the next yard except it hit the tip of the flagpole and dropped precipitously at the foot of Old Glory. From that day on, a ball hit into that yard went from a home run to an automatic out. Our baseball games in the alley were played on a rather narrow but very long "diamond." Home plate was scratched out in the gravel behind our garage. Johnson's garbage can was first base, any available tin can or empty cereal box was second and Willie's garbage can was third base. A field perhaps more accommodating of the football games we would begin when the leaves started turning color.

"I found a hole in his fence. I can reach right through. Come on, I'll show you." Melon turned and ambled towards the corner.

"Gene Autry is going to be in the parade tomorrow," I said.

"Gene Autry? From the movies? Nah....you're nuts....he's not coming to this two-bit dump. Why would he come here from Hollywood? Who told you that?" Melon pounded a fist down on the top of my head to drive home the point. Melonhead is the only person I've ever known who used his fists like punctuation points.

"Lucky Joe, he just told me...."

"Like that old bum would know. What'd he read it in some fish wrapper he pulled out of the trash?"

I was too embarrassed to tell Melonhead that Lucky Joe had invited Gene to the parade and I didn't want to risk that ham hock fist of his coming down on my head once more. We reached the tall Johnson fence just as he finished the last bite of rhubarb. He got down on his knees and pushed the bottom of the fence forward. I joined him on the ground and peered into the forbidden yard. Flowers bloomed everywhere. They had no children to trample the garden. My mother had a small plot full of peonies, although they happened to lie below where we kids jumped from our garage roof. Our landing zone trumped her blossoms.

I felt a weak kick to my rear. I bumped my head on the fence as I was forced ahead. "Hey what are you two boys doing there?" a curiously-affected adult voice demanded. I turned… it was my brother, Mike, testing his vocal chords and authority as an aspiring adult.

Switching to his natural adolescent tenor, "Come on, Ma gave me money and wants us to get haircuts for the parade – said we look like Gypsies."

My brother being a blonde Nordic hardly could be described as such. I suppose she meant we were falling below the lofty standards for male fashion established by unimpeachable sources such as *Boy's Life* and *The Cub Scout Handbook*. She would see to it that we washed twice a day and while we were poor, we were refreshingly clean. I stood and saw that Melonhead was still on his hands and knees. Emboldened by my older brother's presence, I couldn't resist and jumped astride his back like a bronc rider. He was a big boy with a big head….maybe not much in it, but big…and he could buck like a Cayuse in a cactus patch. I wrapped my legs around his ample waist or at least half way around and hung on with one hand on his shirt collar. A few more bucks and he stood and shook like a wet Labrador. I tumbled hard onto the weedy ground. I looked up at my brother who was holding Melonhead at bay with a glare he had been gifted with at birth. The freckled faced boy tried to ignore Mike and hissed in my direction, "Why you little bastard…" That curse would have earned him a mouth washing had his devout Catholic mother heard. I lay on my back, legs upright and cocked in case he broke away from my protector. Then my brother took a quick step toward him and as fast as he came to anger, he settled and the grin returned. I was safe.

"Gene Autry's coming to town, he's going to be in the parade. Lucky Joe said it was so and he invited Gene." I blurted out the news while still on the ground. I worshipped Gene, Roy Rodgers, and even Hop-a-Long despite the mystery of his black hat. And now Gene was coming to town and would be leading our parade. Or so Lucky Joe and I believed.

Distracted by the sincerity in my proclamation, Mike turned his stare from Melonhead to protest, "He ain't coming here. Why would he come all the way from his ranch to see us? I'd heard from Sherry if he were coming. She knows everything that is happening in town…"

"So does Lucky Joe…"

Mike gave a playful kick to the bottom of my worn Keds. "Let's go, Mom gave me some extra money for firecrackers."

Firecrackers, the Fourth of July, I'd almost forgot in my excitement over my favorite cowboy. The 4th was right up there with Halloween, the Last

Day of School, and Christmas. We had a calendar different than our parents. They worshipped the First Day of School; we favored the last day. They celebrated their anniversary; we had our birthdays. We dreamed of the start of baseball season; they were still worried about paying off debts from the Christmas season. As for the Fourth of July, my mother began fretting in June that the next one would be the year we would blow our fingers off, set the house on fire, and fail to have the grass mowed when the parade passed by. The Old Man began complaining in June about another pointless celebration contrived only to hasten his inevitable passage into the county poor house. We shared none of these concerns. In fact, we'd never seen the lawn when it wasn't trimmed and had no idea where the house for poor people was or how it could be different from ours. We just knew we had a right if not an obligation to celebrate Independence Day as patriotic American children who appreciated loud explosions and parades.

In Mandan, a small town in North Dakota that touted itself as 'Where the West Began,' Independence Day, known more fondly as the 4th, was celebrated with the annual parade through Main Street. A world-class rodeo followed and then the American Legion sponsored a fireworks show at night. With all of that pomp and pageantry, who knew... maybe this year the big shots at the Legion got Gene. They could have – the Old Man said the commander at the Legion was a Colonel who served with General Patton. The Old Man to the legion commander to Patton to Gene—not that impossible.

I pushed to my feet and tried to dust myself off only to realize my hands were dirtier than my pants. We turned in unison and left Melonhead in the dust with about six inches remaining on the rhubarb stalk he found more engaging than anything a conversation would offer him. We mounted the bikes Uncle Bill had cobbled together for us in his little basement shop and began the trip downtown, past Bernie's Standard station, the creamery, and down Main Street. We stopped for a moment to see if Melon had taken up the chase out of a delayed realization that he had just been exploited as a source of amusement. He was well-hidden if he was trailing us. Deciding we were well out of the range of Melonhead or the slingshot he usually carried and recklessly used, we filled our cheeks with sunflower seeds and resumed the ride. Trailers with rough stock sped past towards the rodeo grounds. Enormous Brahma bulls eyed us as they rode by. They left a pleasant lingering smell of livestock manure as they moved towards the games. Grandpa Swanson, a pioneer rancher, told me when I once complained of the smell of manure, "That's the smell of money, son."

"What do you think a bastard is?" I asked as I spit out the first split sunflower shells.

"Is that what he said?"

"I think so."

"Beats me, we'll ask him tonight. Let's go."

We moved on past the grocery store and the movie theater. *Pork Chop Hill* was playing. It had been for a few weeks. They had one screen and a slow turnover. Didn't matter as a nickel would get us in and if it was a Western, it was worth seeing a few times. I saw *Tumbling Tumbleweeds* six times.

"There he is…." I pointed down the block. In front of Snowball's bar, a shiny Cadillac stood curbside. Three tall cowboys, not working cowboys, but dudes dressed in their dancing clothes, were coming out of the little corner bar and headed for the long black sedan. "It's Gene Autry." I pedaled hard and then harder to get to him. I was about a half block then less when the three crawled into the back seat and then it was gone. Might as well been a UFO, and not even that could be verified unless Mike saw it too, and he certainly didn't think it was Gene I saw. I'm not sure he was even looking at the right men as the streets were beginning to fill with cowboys and ranchers with ladies on their arms come to town to shop and rodeo.

I'd been through believing in Santa, so I knew enough to not press my point too hard. I'd seen what I'd seen. I still stung from losing the argument in support of the Easter Bunny. It was hard to have an older brother who'd found out life's lessons a few years ahead.

We weaved between the cowboys and their gals and dogs, finally giving up and walking our fat tired bikes to the red and white pole outside of Turner's barber shop. I wasn't so excited to sit in the shop since we boys had found a *Playboy* in Uncle Billy's basement. Up until then, the *National Geographic* at the barber's had offered a rare glimpse at a thin, topless woman who didn't inspire the same stirrings I felt after spending some time with a naked Marilyn Monroe.

Mr. Turner was sitting in his chair, eyes closed. I looked to my brother for a signal that we should chance waking him. Or worse, maybe discover he was dead. Neither, as it turned out… he mumbled, "Come in boys. Have a seat. I'll be right back." He was out the door before we sat. *Sports Afield, Outdoor Life, Look, Life* –a vast array of fine literature to select from—ah, there it is, a *True Detective* that looked as if it held some potential. I settled into the folding metal chair trying to assume the same nonchalance with which I'd read an Archie comic. The place smelled of pomade and shaving lotions. Patsy Cline sang about falling to pieces in husky tones on a scratchy radio nestled behind the counter. Maybe a storm coming this way what with the radio being so full of static. The worn wood counter was covered with scissors, combs, clippers, and bottles of smelly stuff Mr. Turner never wasted on us kids. A stuffed antelope with a broken horn looked over my shoulder from his perch on the paneled wall.

True to his word, Mr. Turner returned promptly. He pointed to me and motioned to the chair. I climbed into the tired leather chair proud that I no longer needed the piece of wood that held the children high enough for Mr. Turner to reach. "How do you want it cut, Sonny?"

"Mom wants him to have a heinie… take it all off she said." My brother, who wore a more fashionable flat-top was just passing along her instructions. The closer he cut the hair the fewer visits I would need. This one would last until after school started.

"Are you boys going to watch the parade tomorrow?" Mr. Turner asked making small talk that barbers are so skilled at.

"Both of us are marching with the Greenbergs baseball team," Mike answered.

"And Gene Autry is leading the parade…" I added without finishing the story.

"Oh, I hadn't heard that. I think that would be front page news. Look at the flyer over there on the wall announcing the parade and the rodeo. You see anything about Gene Autry on there?" He pointed his clippers to a wall filled with posters advertising ranch auctions and dances. I focused on the red, white, and blue parade poster. Mr. Turner was right, Gene wasn't mentioned. That ended the matter. With adults, if it wasn't written, it didn't exist. But Mr. Turner hadn't heard Mr. Joe's story, not that it would have mattered.

Mr. Turner moved close and tossed an apron over my chest then fastened a noose of tissue around my neck either to prevent trimmings from going down my shirt or to serve as a tourniquet should his unsteady hand cause more than the usual nicks and scrapes. His breath smelled the same as the Old Man's when he came home from an evening of reviewing current events with the fellows at the Legion or Snowball's. Evidently Mr. Turner had gone next door to the Black Bull Saloon to bolster the patience he would need to shave nearly bare another moving target. The silver haired man selected an electric trimmer and a number two guard, least that's what he said he was going to use…a number two. The first pass from the bottom towards the top of my large round head was a bad beginning.

"Damn. Your hair is so thick it's clogged my clippers. Damn."

While he was angry, I was in agony. The clippers was stuck and pulling the hair on the back of my neck like he'd set my paper collar on fire. He pulled and tugged and I screamed like the woman in *13 Ghosts*. Finally, he grabbed a scissors and cut the clippers free. My brother had come to my side, although there was little he could do to help.

"Maybe you should just use the scissor, Mister Turner. He ruined the clippers at the other barbers, too. His hair is just too thick."

"I should charge you double," threatened the old barber before returning to his work with a fury rarely seen outside of a fistfight or a television preacher.

My hair flew on the white apron and covered the checkered floor. He had abandoned the clippers and was chopping away with scissors like he was giving a trim to a bear on the run. When it was finally over, I sneezed out some of the clippings and I breathed a sigh of relief. To make it seem like he'd done a fine job after all, the red-faced barber brushed my nose and forehead with the powdered bristled brush then undid the collar he'd fastened around my neck. I scrambled out of the chair as soon as the apron was removed.

"I'll wait outside," I said and scampered out into the heat. A few thunder clouds had moved in during my ordeal and some well spaced but large rain drops hit near my bike where I sat and waited. I hoped to see the shiny Cadillac drive past. A lot of rusty pickups and a few black sedans but no Gene Autry. It wasn't long before Mike strutted out of the shop looking like he'd stepped out of the poster Mr. Turner displayed of the more "modern" styles for young men. Hair so flat and stiff with Butch Wax that a buffalo nickel would have sat up there as if on a pool table. He wore a smile. "Mr. Turner said you should go back to your old barber next time."

"He's an old bastard." I picked up my bicycle and pushed off more than a little hurt that a barber could be so mean and my hair could be so thick. The further from the shop and the closer to the fireworks stand the less ill I felt towards Mr. Turner and the hair I would come to appreciate more as others lost theirs and I still had plenty to spare. We pedaled over the muddy

Cannonball River out towards the old Calvary Post past Buddie's pony rides. The old ponies were harnessed to a merry-go-round for horses. Round and Round and Round all day long with little kids kicking their flanks and pulling on the reins yelling giddy-up and bouncing in the saddle. There must be a special place in heaven for Buddie's Ponies. Or maybe they get reincarnated as nuns and get to slap kids' hands with rulers.

The fireworks 'store' was a ramshackle shack which was open for a few weeks every summer. A pretty woman sat on a tall stool behind the counter. She was a gym teacher at the high school. I'd seen her at the Braves basketball game. "What'll you boys have?" She had a smile just like the smile Marilyn wore on the cover of Uncle Bill's magazine. I was too shy to say what I wanted and couldn't really remember anyway. Mike took over.

"We want Lady Fingers, Black Cats, Sparklers, Snakes, and Cherry Bombs."

"You boys a little young for Cherry Bombs and Black Cats?"

"Okay….give us the rest, then." He knew this was going to be a losing battle and gave up quickly. We'd heard countless warnings from our parents about the lethal potential of Cherry Bombs and suspected this was one cautionary that might be true. Besides Melon would have a whole arsenal if his older brothers were feeling generous. Better he should blow his arms across the Missouri into Bismarck.

We traded a few coins for the stash of fireworks and said goodbye, least my brother said goodbye, I was still too bashful.

We were maybe a block away when I remembered, "Punks, we forgot punks."

"You can wait here if you want. I'll go back and get a few." Mike took off without waiting for a reply. I pulled my heavy cruiser into the shade. Looking off into the hills, I could see where the Indian families had settled into homes which were little more than boxes. Some were actually big refrigerator boxes covered with black tar paper. My mother was the public health nurse for the county and she'd visit these families on a regular basis. She'd make my brother and me pray for the poor souls at bedtime. We always had to plead for mercy for the poor and the sick. She saw to that. Lucky Joe had a shack somewhere up the hillside, least I thought he did.

"Come on, Miss Johnson gave me six punks." Mike pushed past me without stopping heading back towards the Cannonball River Bridge. Pigeons flew out from the metal spans as we crossed the rough timbers. The river smelled skunky, even rancid, as it slowed to a trickle by mid-summer, revealing the perfectly round rocks resembling cannonballs. I kept my eyes peeled for the Cadillac as we pulled back into downtown. I should have kept my eyes on the sidewalk because it was too late when Mike called out a warning. My front tire hit the wood limb spread across the walk. My bike stopped and I went over the top. The third time this week and it was only Thursday. I landed in a roll and back on my feet. I was perfecting this technique. Perhaps I would live to see eleven.

"It's Lucky Joe's brother." Mike pointed to the lifeless body wedged between the lumberyard buildings. I'd run over Lucky Joe's brother's leg. It was wood. I heard the Old Man tell Mom that Lucky and his brother had been war heroes. I didn't know his name except that he was Joe's brother and he'd had his leg blown off by a mine, or so the Old Man had said. Mom said that Lucky was headed for college, but he enlisted in the Army Air Corp to defend America. He could have returned and the government would have paid for his tuition. Instead he came back to Mandan to take care of his brother.

"Is he dead? Did I kill him?" I asked as I crept closer. He lay on his stomach between the buildings. I moved closer. He smelled like Mr. Turner's breath.

"I think he's just drunk and passed out."

"You sure I didn't kill him when I hit him?"

"No, I'm not sure, but he was lying there already when I shouted for you to watch out. I don't think you hurt him."

Just then, he grunted and rolled ever so slightly. Then he groaned, rolled over and sat up. We stared until we recovered our senses. Then we panicked as one and made a getaway on the rusty bikes. My fender rubbed on the balloon tire causing a noisy and slow retreat. Two blocks later, we stopped. Mike pulled the fender from the tire and we set out for home. It had been a stressful day and a few hours of blowing things up before supper would be a satisfying way to end the day. Like the Old Man told Mom, 'A guy's got blow off a little steam.'

Willie, and his sister Sherry, were huddled beside Melon who was bent over a tin can. We approached up the alley. The trio jumped back from the can and a second later it flew into the air, higher than Johnson's waving flag. Cherry bomb or M-80, could have been either. Melonhead's older brothers came through again. The fireworks were starting a day early this year… likely a sign of post-war prosperity. It would be a loud evening and nothing would be safe, not the garbage cans, milk boxes, and particularly not the ant hills. Ants must despise the 4th. We planted cherry bombs and strings of Black Cats and filled the holes. In the very long and successful history of insects, few bugs suffered as much as our neighborhood ants. Well, maybe the gophers had it as bad. We'd crawl on our stomachs like soldiers moving on an enemy pillbox and plant the explosives in the hole. Our punks at ready, we'd light the fuses and rush for cover. I never saw any injured gopher, although it wasn't hard to imagine a few furry little fellows cowering in their caves with singed pelts. I still ask for redemption and can only hope they've forgiven me for my youthful fascination with explosives.

The bell at the First Lutheran Church rang six times. We atomized one more ant hill then followed the aroma of hot dogs and baked beans to our cozy kitchen. Mom gave us each a hug and sent us to the sink to wash our filthy paws – explosive demolition was dirty work. The Old Man was already at the table. It was his day off from the railroad where he was a switchman. I never knew exactly what he did when he left our house with a silver metal lunch box and a switchman's lantern off to work five days a week. Mike and I joined them at the table and bowed over folded hands for grace. Mom could be inspired to draw that into a sermon if it was a particularly rough or happy day. More than once we witnessed a hot meal become cold leftovers as she offered thanks for everything and asked mercy for everyone.

That accomplished, we undertook to assemble our hot dogs according to our respective tastes with a harmony that comes only with years of eating together and knowing the extent of one's own reach and the next person's patience. The garnishes were the product of the Old Man's garden which he kept out by the river. It provided a few small cucumbers not worth the trouble of pickling and a small pail of half-ripe tomatoes.

While we dined, Mike and I gave an account of our activities since we departed after breakfast leaving out the events that might have caused a scolding. In our younger more naïve years, we shared everything. We, well my brother, caught on that we needed to filter the accounts—a lesson that later served me well as an employee who had to report to a boss who, unlike my mother, didn't comfort me with a hug after the reprimand.

"Gene Autry is coming to town. He's leading the parade tomorrow. Lucky Joe told me…"

The Old Man had finished eating and was washing dishes when I mentioned this in hopes of gaining confirmation. "You and Lucky Joe must be the only two in town who Gene told."

The Old Man had a sly Norwegian style of understated humor. I never understood that until I was twenty-something. I took him literally and thought it best to drop the matter. Maybe Lucky Joe had been teasing me, too. He was a great tease and a better storyteller. Sometimes when I would bring him food or maybe some underwear or socks I thought the Old Man wouldn't miss, he'd tell stories of his ancestors who lived in the village of earth huts north of town. He said his people remember when Louis and Clark came and spent the winter. He said they were good men and welcomed guests who left behind many babies. I remember being confused about Lucky Joe's amusement over the proliferation of children...what did that have to do with adventure and exploring? Years later, it occurred to me that it was a long cold winter huddled under the buffalo robes in the great earthen huts and it was comforting to know that friendly commerce went beyond exchanging dry goods and furs.

Summer was great because it extended outside play hours until well after nine. This evening, instead of kick the can, pump-pump pull away, or alley ball, we returned to our stash of fireworks. I spent a few frustrating minutes trying to direct the burning of the little black pyramids we called "snakes" as they contorted into every shape but for the one I wanted and then they disintegrated into dust at the touch of a finger....a true lesson on life. Then, as it grew dark, the sparklers came out. All the neighborhood kids ran from yard to yard holding flashing sparklers over their heads. Sparks flew and burned little holes in our shirts. Finally, we turned our attention towards Snake Hill where the Goldbergs shot off the few biggest and most expensive fireworks. The ones the Old Man refused to purchase based upon his seemingly unreasonable contention that it was money gone up in smoke—a view he and I now share. The Goldberg extravaganza lasted only a few minutes but still demanded our attention and inspired a few oohs and ahs. It also signaled the end of the day and we dragged ourselves to bed, dog-tired with the rocket's red glare and visions of sparklers still dancing in our heads.

The Fourth of July parade started at ten in the morning. It was sunny and already 85 as our baseball team, Greenbergs, queued up behind the Greenberg's float. A couple of last year's homecoming queens stood on the otherwise unremarkable float which was in fact a hay wagon decorated sparingly with green crepe paper. We didn't have a team name like the bulldogs or the demons…they just called us Greenbergs because Mr. Greenberg bought the green ball caps that distinguished us as a team. We didn't have age groups. Team members were from seven to Bobby Grindle who was at least sixteen although still in the sixth grade so he qualified. Bobby gave us some real Babe Ruth batting power, but the center fielder had to cover Bobby's right field too because Bobby moved with the speed and course of a bike with a flat.

The First Lutheran Church bell rang ten times and the fire engine which started and led the parade turned on its weak wailing siren. The Greenberg float took off with a start. A bright green John Deere Model B pulled the wagon and when the rancher/driver, more accustomed to hauling hay bales than beauty queens, let out the clutch he neglected to allow for the queens' court all of whom tumbled to the wagon floor. The Greenbergs cheered at the sight. We followed behind skipping or walking and throwing our balls or gloves in the air and making catches that we imagined had won the World Series.

I never saw the front of the parade. By the time we reached the end point in front of the Black Bull Bar, the parade was pretty much over except for a few horse riders and the guys picking up the manure left by the horses who preceded us. As kids in a Western town, we didn't view the manure as a nuisance so much as an opportunity to jump on the still-steamy mounds causing it to spurt up on the pants of whichever kid wasn't quick or bright enough to move. The novelty of the first splatter quickly disappeared as we began to notice the accumulation on our shoes. Slowly we formed a weary troop heading back to the neighborhood. My fatigue wasn't due so much to the parade marching as it was to the weight of holding up hope that Gene Autry would appear somehow, somewhere…and then…he hadn't. The only light on an otherwise gloomy horizon was the rodeo that would kick off that evening. I'd rather watch the toothless and scarred bull riders more than almost anything except for Miss Martin writing on the chalkboard or Marilyn posing in a magazine.

Mike and I abandoned the fireworks for the remainder of the day, instead meeting in the alley after returning home to dump our gloves and green hats. I changed into jeans, cowboy boots and a wide brim hat that Mom had stuffed with old socks so it would fit my head. It had been her grandfather's hat when he was a rancher south of Simms. We waited in the alley for Melonhead. When he showed, he was wearing a complete cowboy outfit, hat, bandana, vest, chaps, boots and spurs that jingled when he walked. Never before had we seen one of our own like this.

"Where did you get that get-up?" Willie asked.

"My Uncle George brought it. He's in the rodeo, a bronc buster. He's from Billings and he bought it for me. He's even going to get me back in the holding pens with the real cowboys. He said I should look like I belong there."

"You look like a rodeo clown," Mike said.

So taken with his new duds and prized position with the rodeo stars was he that Melonhead didn't even nibble at the bait. Or maybe he didn't want to soil the dandy outfit with an all out fight in the dirt. He just left, walking down the alley towards Ohm's Café. Willie and I just followed.

"Come on we're gonna miss the good stuff." By the viaduct, we all caught up with Melon and had mostly forgotten his appearance until some hoods with greasy ducktails shouted from a passing car that Melonhead should 'Get a horse.' I had to admit, that the addition of a horse might help justify his lavish appearance.

Over the railroad bridge, down across the lazy Cannonball River, past the park, and to the fairgrounds we tramped listening to Melonhead's spurs jingle as we were mostly quiet. It was as though we'd allowed a foreigner in our midst and we weren't certain if that should alter our behavior. New pack norms had to be established.

We could smell the rodeo grounds before we could see it nestled in the bowl surrounded by tall cottonwood trees. Then we could hear the livestock mostly horses, calves, and bulls bellowing for each other's attention or out of pure excitement. They knew what was coming. The calves knew they would be wrestled to the ground by flying cowboys or roped and tied for a few seconds. The bulls and broncs knew that rough men with sharp metal on their boots would straddle them and try to stay on their backs if only for a few seconds. The air was full of anticipation. The high school band played songs familiar although unnamed to us. Vendors selling cotton candy, soda, and popcorn shouted as we passed by. Melonhead stopped at a new vendor. She was selling Fizzies, a small tablet you could drop in a glass of water that would produce the most marvelous carbonated root beer. He ordered one and got a cup of water. The tablet sprung to life as it hit the water. He drank three quarters of the liquid then passed it for us to share. Tasted like someone threw a handful of aspirin in a can of stale beer and tree bark and it was probably just as toxic.

The band struck up *Back in the Saddle* as a prelude to *The Star Spangled Banner* and we ran to the rear of the arena where the shoots where loaded with rodeo stock. Cowboys everywhere, though none dressed as fancy as Melonhead. He picked up the pace when he spotted his uncle – running clumsily in boots too large his spurs whirled. We stayed a few steps behind out of deference. After all it was Melonhead's day to shine. Sure enough his uncle led him away and when last seen he was perched on the fence next to the pens holding the Appaloosa broncs. We admired him for a brief time then shuffled off to find seats with the common folks.

"Little Moose."

I heard my name called. Only one person called me 'Little Moose.' To the rest of the world just 'Moose' would do.

I turned to greet Lucky Joe. He was wearing a new western shirt with metal buttons and clean jeans over some dusty cowboy boots. He even had a straw cowboy hat instead of the scruffy Mandan Braves cap he normally wore. In fact, Lucky Joe looked like the real Westerner Melonhead had wanted to become.

"Come with me. There is something we must do." I looked at my brother, shrugged and bowed my head as I dutifully followed Lucky Joe. We walked past the chutes. I stole a glance at Melon perched on the fence. He looked my way. His grin revealed an arrogant pride more typical of crooked politicians.

....

Almost fifty years later, I look at the yellow newspaper clipping and still feel the emotions. The photograph shows a boy wearing an enormous brimmed hat riding on the back of a horse named Champion. The cowboy held reins in his left hand and the American flag in his right hand. The caption below the photograph reads, "Gene Autry and an unidentified boy led the opening ceremonies at the Mandan Rodeo." Ridin' tall next to Gene and me is my pal Lucky Joe, the man who had been Gene's crewmate as they flew their missions over China and Burma. Life in the West was good and while Mr. Joe had the name Lucky, I realized that it was me who was lucky to have Mr. Joe as a friend. It was me who learned that day to judge folks by their heart and not their station in life. Mr. Joe, he had a good heart.

Becoming Zindelo

"A forty-eight Caddy."

"A fifty-five Chevy."

"A fifty-one Dodge, and I got a straight flush. A fifty-one, two, three, four, and five Dodge!" I shouted hoarsely. It was my birthday, and I'd been shouting to the world since blowing out the candles at noon. We'd become so raucous that the Old Man ordered us outside. Those of us not quick enough to the porch swing had to settle into the wooden high-back rockers the old folks seemed to favor. We'd intended to play a cut-throat hand or two of Old Maid, but after the last game, two days ago, Mickey had inadvertently disappeared with the queens. So we combined another favorite activity, identifying the models of cars driving down 6th Avenue, with poker as we understood it. With those hybrid rules in play, we could make a flush by spotting five Fords or as I had just done a straight flush combining the make and year. A rare feat, still it was my birthday, and anything was possible on your birthday. After all it was your Day.

"Where were you born?" Sherry asked me when the game ended and we moved off the porch onto the thick, green grass dotted with the yellow dandelions that seemed to thrive on the carcinogenic herbicide the Old Man doused them with.

"In Mandan, I guess. I don't know, I don't remember."

"He wasn't 'born,' we found him in a pumpkin patch. I was there when they picked him," my brother, Mike, interjected with the privilege of the first born and an elder. I didn't fully believe it, although life was full of surprises every day. Who could have imagined a mamba snake capable of biting to death an entire village in one vengeful rampage, or a mummy trundling its way to North Dakota to exact a toll against our neighborhood to keep up his end of a curse? Frogs started out as tadpoles; caterpillars turned into butterflies. It wasn't impossible that my beginnings could have been in the form of a small gourd.

The six of us, all neighborhood friends, lay still on the lawn, watching the billowing clouds animate themselves into forms, evaporate, and become something new—ends and beginnings; birth and death. Where did they begin? Where did they go? Our stomachs were happily topped with chocolate cake, vanilla ice cream, and grape Kool-Aid. Mickey still sported a rather dashing purple mustache that resembled Clark Gable's in form if not in color. But "the question" kept appearing with every new shape of a cloud and I couldn't let go without understanding.

"If I was 'found' then why is today my *birth*day? It should be my *found*-day or something like that."

"You don't know what you're talking about. Today is the..."

"I do, too. Today is the day, I popped out of Mom's tummy..."

"You didn't just pop out," Mike said with all of the authority of a medical doctor.

"I know I did because mom showed me the scar."

"I did too," Willie added. The more information I got, the more confused I became. Still, I also knew that I was now on a quest to my origins, or more accurately the source of my existence.

"You two don't even know how you were made," Mike continued to taunt us without offering much in the way of explanation. While I was reasonably certain about the process of my birth which had been explained by our neighbor, Mary, who was almost a nurse, Mike was right. I didn't have the lowdown on my humble creation. We'd all gotten the story about planting seeds, but I'd seen the Old Man planting his carrots and rutabaga seeds and frankly, I failed to sense a nexus.

"You boys shouldn't be talking about..." Sherry pouted.

Mike sat up abruptly and interrupted, "You get here when your dad makes love to your mother."

"What's making love?" I asked innocently but with growing curiosity. Finally, I might learn the secret of my creation.

"Mike, get in here and get dressed, Valerie's father will be arriving in ten minutes to take you to the dance," my mother's melodic voice sang out through the screen door. "And you kids should probably get home. Your mothers will be expecting you. The party is over."

Mike sprang to his feet, off for his first 'date' although it wasn't called that, leaving us none the more enlightened about making love. Planting seeds, making love, none of this was adding up. Was it something my brother would be looking into with Valerie tonight?

The others drifted off and soon it was just Mickey and me watching the clouds transfigure into horses, buffalo, and even an enormous heart that seemed to shade our entire town. "Do you know about making love?"

I suspected Mickey possessed the answer. He often did but was seldom forthcoming with a simple explanation. "Those clouds could tell us," was all I got as he floated to his feet and moved away so quickly, I ran to catch up. He tread so lightly his sneakers barely touched the sidewalk, past the lilac bushes, and down the gravel alley where the McCormick's garbage can smelled of rotting fish. Without further conversation, we arrived at Melonhead's back steps. In the shade, there sat the tubby boy, face dusted with freckles matching his pumpkin colored locks, spitting sunflower seeds at the calico cat snoozing at his feet.

As if approaching the oracle of the Dakotas, Mickey and I, bowed slightly at the waist and waited for him to acknowledge our presence and speak. It didn't take long. "Whaddya want you little goof?" He spit the words out with a slug of seeds at our shoes instead of the cat's head. Not the greeting one would hope for from such a sage.

"What does making love mean?" I asked respectfully and took a step back to dodge the onslaught of seeds which filled his cheeks like a starving chipmunk. He could spit them with the speed and velocity of a Gatling gun.

"It's what your old man does to your old lady. You two are too young and stupid to know about that."

Now we were getting somewhere. "But what is it that he does?" I asked believing that he wouldn't give up the knowledge without some prodding. I didn't like groveling before this oaf, but I liked not knowing about procreation even less.

"It's when he puts his dingus into her dingus and spits you out. You grow to about as big as watermelon in her stomach." He adjusted his aim and shot a salvo of seeds between my legs. "Then she poops you out and that's why you're such a turd. Now, get lost!" He stood in case he'd have to enforce his order with a pounding.

I opened my mouth to push a little harder, but Mickey, being the wiser had already rounded the porch corner and Melonhead had already taken two steps down. The calico cat sensing the next step would be on him, dashed away. I took it as an omen and joined the tomcat and Mickey in retreat. Melonhead flung a few more curses. I failed to comprehend the words as his mouth was too full although his intent was clear.

When I caught up to Mickey, he simply offered, "Sometimes you have to suffer through many false prophets before you find the truth."

Sometimes, a guy's brain just needs nourishment to clear his mind and formulate a plan and I had a few crisp dollar bills fresh from my party just burning a hole in my jeans pocket. "Let's go to Ohm's," I suggested to Mickey who seemed to have read my mind and was pointed in that direction. We traveled in the alley. We always did even if the street was easier. So did the neighbor dogs. Except for the McAllister's garbage cans, the alley was less congested and less visible to scrutiny by parents and neighbors looking out of windows. Since it also doubled as a very narrow baseball diamond and a very long football field, we all knew it intimately and sometimes got a closer look at the graveled surface than we really needed. Still, it was ours and it got us places quickly.

I smelled the burger cafe before I could see it. The breeze carried the addictive aroma of frying hamburgers and French fries down the alley and into my nose until my mouth watered. I could have traveled there with my eyes closed, just following the delicious scent. I believe as a soul approaches St. Peter's Gate, the aroma of Ohm's burgers will be there to greet you. Little did I know then that it would be a memory for a lifetime. With two hands and a shoulder, I threw open the heavy metal back door. The place was empty, save a tired looking cowboy nursing a cup of coffee in both hands. We dived in a booth and Mickey toyed with the jukebox selector. *Bye, Bye, Love, For Your Precious Love, Love Letters in the Sand, Love Potion No. 9*, Mickey read from the list of songs in the jukebox. We were surrounded by love. This might be the right place to find out about making love.

"What can I get ya?" the waitress startled me when she gave my hair a tussle with her bright red fingernails.

"Hi, Frankie, what do you know about making love?" I blurted out with a naïve sense of propriety.

"Love making? I guess I'm an expert. Mostly with fall'n in love. Actually, with fall'n out of love, too. One usually follows the other."

"But what about making love?"

She nestled her rawboned frame next to me. She smelled like Aunt Tillie's special perfume on a Sunday morning. She played with her auburn hair, twisting it around her long fingers and looked me in the eye. "Moose, I've had my share of making love, some of the old bitties would say more than my share. It's when you find someone you're really attracted to and well, then things just sorta take their natural course."

"But how do you do it? How do you make love?" Out of the corner of my eye, I could see Mickey still paging through the song selections as though he knew the answer but would be patient while I persisted.

"Well, I usually start with hold'n hands, then maybe a little hugg'n and then a kiss and if the kiss is just right, well then things go on from there."

"What things? Where do you go from there?" I was getting close. I could feel the answer coming with her next breath.

"How 'bout some more coffee there, darling?" the cowboy growled with a voice choked with grit and gravel.

"Hold your horses, Sam, Moose here is gett'n a lesson on making love."

"How 'bout I take the little man down to Bobbi Jo's? That'll give him a hell of a lesson on making love."

"Who's Bobbi Jo?"

Frankie slid from the booth wearing a smile that highlighted her buckteeth and framed by lips smeared with thick red lipstick. "I best get him some coffee before this here conversation gets out of hand. Moose, what can I bring you?"

"A chocolate malted would be nice, thank you, ma'am."

'They say that for every boy and girl, there is just one love in this whole world,' Tab Hunter crooned *Young Love* through the jukebox silver speakers. I sucked the thick chocolate concoction through the thin paper straw. Just one love? How was I to find her? Just one girl in the whole world? How will I know which one? Who would love me?

Seems Frankie was still searching for hers and I was still looking for answers. It was like when the Pastor spoke of the Holy Spirit. Everyone nodded and recited their belief, however getting an answer as to what he looked like or where he hung out had eluded me.

When we left the café, Frankie was leaning across the counter talking softly to Sam. Maybe Sam would be the one she was searching for. Mickey had been strangely silent and hadn't touched the second straw in the malt. We walked down the cracked sidewalk, aimlessly moving across the viaduct. The aroma of burning wood from below drew us beneath the bridge to hobo camp. Three men sat with their backs to us watching a black pot over a small fire.

"Little Moose come join us." It was Lucky Joe and he twisted his lanky torso to face Mickey and me. A freshly rolled cigarette hung loosely between his lips and wiggled when he spoke. We ambled over to the pot and squatted a respectful distance away. "Come closer, my little friend. This is Harry and this here big boy is Bobby. On their way to Oregon, to pick fruit they say."

Bobby had a welcoming face with big round blue eyes and blonde hair sticking out of his Chicago Cubs' ball cap. "Want to ride the rails with us?"

"Someday, maybe, not today, it's my birthday so it wouldn't be a good day to leave home." Mickey turned to me with a smile that suggested that I'd either made the right call or had really missed the chance of a lifetime.

"Little Moose, I think you are troubled today."

"It's my birthday and my brother told me that I wasn't born and that I was found in a pumpkin patch and then that got us started about where I came from and I said I popped out of my mother's stomach and then Melonhead spit seeds at me and said I was made when my father put his dingus in my mother and spit seeds, and then Frankie told me about holding hands and kissing, and I still don't know where I come from."

"I'm from St. Louis," Harry said. "Bobby here, he's from hell, least that's the way he acts most of the time."

"What'd you guys know about making love?"

"I know I ain't made any for a few years. Women folk ain't much interested in men without any jingle in their pocket," Bobby smiled but looked sad. "How 'bout you, Harry? You been making any love other than wit your own self?"

Harry cursed and slapped the blonde man alongside his head. "Hell, no, can't 'fford to buy it and they ain't given it away to the likes of me. Now if I had a fine suit and a shiny Cadillac, that be a different story. Besides, I won't want no gal that'd have me."

"Joe?"

"Little Moose, that's not a question that you ask a man."

"Why?"

"'Cause he'll either lie to you and say he has when he ain't or say he has-n't when he be gett'n it on the sly." The ash on the cigarette had burned almost to his lips without a single bit falling. "And answering that question doesn't respect our women and the mothers of our children."

"But I don't even know what you're talking about. What is making love? Where do I come from and please don't talk about planting gardens, I'm beginning to doubt that's true."

"Rhonda Little Hawk and I, we used to make sweet music together." Lucky Joe stared into the sky as if enjoying the memory.

"You sing or play the guitar…"

"No, boy, making love is like making music together." Lucky Joe leaned towards me and looked as if he was about to finally share the facts that all adults seemed to be holding close. "Me and Rhonda, we'd go to the top of Buffalo Ridge, where the cedars grow and shade the sweetgrass. She'd bring her finest blanket and we lay together, just feeling each other's warmth, each other's spirit."

"Didn't ya get hot? I mean hanging on to each other in the summer?"

The dark haired man laughed until he rolled off his apple crate onto the dirt. When he regained his composure, he pointed at me with a long dirty finger, "Boy, they didn't have no clothes on, they's buck naked when they's making love."

"That true, Joe, were you buck naked?"

"That we were Little Moose, not a stitch to get between us. Now that's all I've got to tell you about this matter." His cigarette finally burned to his parched lips and he tossed it towards the rails.

I soaked in the odor of fresh creosote from the new railroad ties and the idea that Joe and the Little Hawk woman were naked in the sweetgrass. "Then what'd you do?"

Lucky Joe stood abruptly. "I am not an expert on lovemaking, but I know some folks who are. How about we walk over and talk with them?" With-out waiting for an answer, he turned on his heels and began to walk towards the Cannonball River. Mickey and I skipped behind trusting that our pal was likely to take us to the top of the mountain where a wise man would reveal the truth that no one else could speak. Joe was a shaman himself so if he had the lowdown on a real expert in lovemaking, it would be the best. "Joe would know how to read the clouds," observed Mickey in a way that linked the moment with earlier parts of the day in a connection only Mickey could make.

We hiked along the slow moving brown water bordered by towering cottonwood trees quaking in the breeze. The winding river led us to a decrepit wooden bridge, which we crossed and then continued on a bare path through a thick growth of dogwood. I kept right on Joe's heels as it would be easy to get lost in the bramble. Finally, we came to a meadow. A dozen or more brightly painted wagons formed a semi-circle in the opening. A few horses, mostly pintos, grazed lazily on the tall grass. A couple of black goats darted through the chickens causing them to take flight and land on the wagons. Music, like I'd never heard before floated across the meadow. With guitars and fiddles, it had a mystical quality, enticing me to come visit. Gypsies.

The music stopped as we neared. The women wore long skirts and bodacious scarves with jewelry – rings on their fingers, their toes, and in both ears. Long, black hair fell down the backs to their waists. The men dressed the same except they wore pants instead of skirts – and big black mustaches. A man with the longest mustache I'd ever seen, broke from the circle and strode towards us, his tall, black boots kicking up miniature dust storms.

"My brother, welcome to our camp," the man spoke with a strong accent, pleasant, still foreign and a bit hard to understand. So difficult, in fact, I hoped I was right that he had said welcome and not to get the hell out of here. He didn't smile so it was hard to tell.

"Besnik, my friend, it's been too long." Besnik and Joe embraced and kissed the side of each other's cheek. I'd never seen men do that. Perhaps some shaman ritual like the secret handshake that Melonhead used to make us perform to enter his basement where he kept forbidden magazines.

"And your friend?" the mustachioed man waved his rough hand towards me.

"This is Little Moose. He's looking for love. He wants to know where he..."

"Joe, my lover, where have you been? We've been here a week. And have you come to visit? No!" The raven haired woman had Joe in her arms, lifted from the ground, and twirled him around like a rag doll. She carried him off past the camp fire and out of sight, leaving me with Bees Knees or whatever Joe had called him.

"So, you're looking for love? You've come to the right place. You will join the Romani. We have plenty of love. Come." He grabbed my arm, before I could retreat to the river. I looked to Mickey for help. He was gone – again. I was on my own.

Besnik ushered me past the campfire where the men had resumed playing their little guitars and fiddles. A few women danced around the fire ring and beat small drums. There were no children and I recalled that Melonhead had told me the gypsies eat kids once they'd eaten all of the dogs. I didn't see any dogs either. An enormous black pot bubbled and steamed over the fire. It emitted an unfamiliar but tantalizing odor.

A large and stunningly beautiful woman sat on fat pillows under a dusty canvas awning strung out from a wagon. "This is Moose, he's looking for love." Besnik gave me a slight shove towards the exotic lady. "Come, sit at my feet. My name is Tshilaba." I walked on my knees to her side, my eyes scanning for an escape route. Mickey was probably watching and waiting in the trees, just out of sight. She poked my ribs with a painted fingernail, checking for fat.

"Moose. What does Moose mean?" She spoke almost without an accent.

"It doesn't mean anything. It's my name. It's who I am. I'm Moose."

"That's your nickname, what's your real name?"

Now, I saw that question as a turning point. Perhaps I won't be eaten. Uncle Herman had been a rancher all of his life and he told me that a guy never wanted to name a steer, 'because then you don't want to eat them.'

"Larry, that's my real name."

"Larry? That's worst than Moose. You're Zindelo from now on." I thought I heard a polite giggle from the trees but knew Mickey could keep a secret—maybe better than anyone ever.

"Zindelo? I'm Zindelo? What does Zindelo mean?"

"It means son."

I'd dodged another one of the bullets life occasionally fired my way. They weren't going to name me 'son' and then put me in the pot.

"Besnik, from now on you will call him Zindelo. Fetch Drina, quickly."

Besnik trotted off towards the fire.

"So, little Zindelo, you're looking for love. Let me see your hand."

I hesitated then shyly offered my left hand. If she was going to keep it, I'd just as soon sacrifice my left one now that I'd learn to throw and write with my right hand. She seized my paw, turned it face up, and studied it. "You have a strong Love Line, my dear, very strong. You will be powerful, rough, and wild with the girl who gets you. She will be very happy with you." That time, I knew I heard a giggle from across the small creek in the woods.

She twisted and tilted my hand in the sunlight. "Ah, you have a deep long Marriage Line. That is good. You will make a good partner. Yes, Zindelo, I approve."

Approve?

Besnik returned with a smile on his face and the prettiest girl I'd ever laid eyes on. "This is Drina, she will be your bride."

Even with his thick accent, I know he said 'your bride.' I looked at Drina…not bad, but not bride material either. There was no way I was going to celebrate my birthday and my wedding on the same day. Drina moved by my side and slipped my hand into hers. It was warm and soft. She walked away from the makeshift tent. Without so much as a slight tug on my hand, I followed. I didn't want to be rude and was just about as curious as I was afraid. She led me to a path beside the unnamed creek coursing to the river. She sat, I sat. She wrapped her arms around my shoulders and pulled me close to her lips. She kissed me. I'd kissed her back although frankly, I didn't know how. Her lips were so soft, so sweet, so unlike anything I'd experienced. She kissed me again this time laying me on my back and crawling on top of my confused self.

At first, I thought it was Mickey who came to my rescue. Not in an orthodox manner such as riding a mustang in a cavalry charge. No, he just made the most haunting sounds like some furious bear. It came from where I'd last seen the woman lead Joe, across the little creek. Drina screamed. I screamed even louder and bounced to my feet. The amour vanished as did Drina, evidence that the fittest, the fastest, would be the one to survive.

Besnik came as fast as Drina had left. These Gypsies were proving to be fleet of foot. "Zindelo, my son, what was it? Drina said a monster got you, her husband to be."

"It ran off, I chased it off to save Drina." I was reaching, but it sounded heroic to me.

"Come, we'll find Joe and tell him of the marriage. I'm so pleased he brought you to us." He moved his big black boots towards the camp.

I mustered up all of the courage I could. More than it took to chase the beast. More than confessing to Mr. Johnson that I'd broken his window for the third time. "Mr. Besnik, I didn't come here to get married. I'm not old enough...I can't get married."

As if I pulled the cougar's tail, Besnik had me in the air by my shirt collar. "You what? You no want my Drina and after you spoiled her and..." Besnik's lips continued to move. I know because my eyes were a half inch away. But I've no hint of what came from them. I could see being Moose again and becoming stew for the colorful folks. They all looked well fed.

"Besnik, calm down, my good friend, Besnik." Not a moment to soon, Lucky Joe came scampering from across the creek, where I'd heard the bear sounds, pulling his shirt over his head.

I fell to the ground like a glop of Jell-O. And then I was back in the tent. Maybe Joe carried me. Maybe Besnik kicked me down the path and into the tent. He still looked furious. Drina perched on a stool in the corner wearing a pout like I'd perfected for every visit to the dentist. Tshilaba studied some leaves on her table. She put them in the palm of her hand, shook them, and dumped the dried leaves on the tabletop.

With great formality and finality, Tshilaba announced, "Moose is not the one for Drina."

My former fiancé ran from the tent sobbing. Never again in my life, would I have a female so forlorn over my departure. It was quite inspiring, at least for a moment.

"Moose, you should leave. You've broken her heart," Tshilaba spoke with authority although without malice.

For the second time today, I summoned courage from the depths of my soul. "I'm sorry, I hurt her feelings. I never came here looking for a wife. I came looking for answers. It's my birthday and I just wanted to know how I came to be here on earth. Everyone tells me something different and Joe said you folks would have the answer."

"That's why you came?" Besnik's face softened. "You want to know how you were made?"

"Yes, that's all."

Besnik hit his forehead with his three-fingered hand. "Zindelo, you come with me."

"Do I have to get married?"

"No, No, just come."

We walked to a red, wooden wagon with gold gilding. Besnik swung open a door more suited for an elf and we crawled in. Joe waited at the doorway for a moment then walked away. It was cramped. I sat on a bench that might have also been a bed. Besnik rummaged in a closet, tossing things on the floor and onto the tables. He opened a massive gold plated chest and dug inside. Finally, he found what he was looking for.

"Close your eyes and give me your hand."

I did and he led me a few steps to the front of the wagon. I squeezed my eyes closed. He placed my hand in what felt like a box. Inside was a soft fur-like object. Smooth and pleasant. My hand rubbed the silkiness.

"Keep your eyes closed. Bring your hand to your nose. Now smell your hand." I did and it was wonderful. It smelled like Drina only better.

Besnik led me back to the seat. "You open your eyes now. But turn your back to me."

I did and could hear him stirring about making noises that didn't provide a clue as to what he was doing. "I'm going to blindfold you." He put a scarf over my eyes and turned me around. He took my hands and placed them on a glass. "Drink this."

I did and it tasted sweet and went down easy, I wanted more but Besnik pulled the glass down and took it from my hands.

"Now do you want to know what you touched and what you drank? Do you really want to know?"

In the darkness of the scarf, my mind screamed, of course, I want to know, but then it occurred to me. Wanting to know is how I almost became married. Did I really want to know?

"Did the liquid taste good?"

I nodded my head.

"And did that feel good to rub?"

"I want to know." I tore off the scarf and on the small table before me was a fur pelt, black with a white stripe, a skunk, I'd rubbed the skunk and thought it wonderful, it even smelled heavenly. And in the glass, was a milky substance with a yellow eye staring up at me.

"That's goat's milk with fresh eggs sweetened with honey. You see, Zindelo, sometimes its best not to know. Sometimes, it's best just to shut your eyes, your mind, and just enjoy!"

"I wished I'd kept the blindfold on." My stomach roiled as I stared at the eggs floating in the goat's milk.

"You want to know where you come from? You know where I come from?"

"No."

"I don't know where I come from. You know why they call us Gypsies? Because some think we are the pharaoh's people from Egypt, so they just call us Gypsy. But they do not know. And some call us Romani because we're from Romania. But they don't know."

"That's not what I mean…"

"I know where you come from because it's where I come from."

Gypsies sure can speak in riddles.

"You and I both come from our fathers' and mothers' love. It was their love that made us. Enjoy that for now. That's all you need to taste for now, your parents' love. You go now."

I climbed down the wooden steps on the back of the wagon, my mind still trying to follow Besnik. Joe was waiting with Drina. The pout had been replaced with the most lovely smile. "We'll be back next year. I'll wait for you to join us then." She embraced me and being a head taller, pulled my head into her bosom. I walked away like a drunken sailor, Joe holding on to my shoulder. I saw two or three Mickeys floating forward to meet us as we moved back into the dogwood.

We tramped over the creaking bridge and took a short-cut to town. I could hear the bells in the church ring six times. The sky had cleared and a stiff wind cut into our faces.

"Did you find what you were looking for?" Joe faced me and pulled a tobacco pouch from his jeans.

"I think so but not how I expected it."

"That is sometimes the way the best answers come."

"I'm sorry I asked so many questions."

"No, Little Moose, a man should always have more questions than answers. The Great Spirit knows of love and the Great Spirit will share it with you when you need it, but you must remember to give it as freely your Self."

Despite my young age, I felt like a man for the first time—sometimes the answer is right there all of the time. I thanked my friend and teacher, Lucky Joe, looked up at the clear blue sky and began the walk home hand-in-hand with my timid pal and the Great Spirit.

. . . .

"Where do I come from, Grandpa? I didn't come from the pumpkin patch, did I?"

My grandson had pestered me for the third time as we sat on the front porch swing watching lightening blaze across the sky. My mind drifted back to Melonhead's explanation and I was tempted to tell him, using more anatomically correct language. Then I thought about what Lucky Joe had told me and how Besnik had shown me that I could find satisfaction without complete knowledge, and how when I did learn 'the facts of life,' how disappointed I'd been.

With innocent bright eyes, the color of a newborn filly, my grandson looked at me and patiently waited for my answer.

"No, you didn't come from the pumpkin patch, you came from a gift God gave your parents. You came from the love between your mother and father. Let that be enough to know for now."

1 Corinthians 13:11

Wearing pigtails tied with yellow ribbons and a smile bigger than her face, Cathy P. paused at the school entrance, poised like a cat waiting for the fat mouse. "Moose, what did you do on summer vacation?"

"Ah, well, we just went ..." I began but was cut off by Miss P. who stood a head taller than me, a fact that in social discourse always seemed to give her the high ground.

"I went to Disneyland and we went through Yellowstone and Yosemite and...."

My wandering mind drifted like a dead cottonwood down the Missouri back to the summer that had just passed. My summer vacation was like that tree. I just drifted through the lazy days filled with friends and of course our yearly family trip. I had mixed feelings about the limitations and humble nature of our vacation. None of our friends had wealth, except the Goldbergs, of course. Still many managed a trip beyond the borders of North Dakota. We'd heard stories of trips to Minneapolis, or the Lakes, and the Grand Canyon. Every year, upon returning to school, the obligatory report on *What I Did on my Summer Vacation* was penned and read aloud by each student.

Cathy P.'s invitation to summarize my vacation and her extravagant unsolicited description of hers was but a hint of what I had yet to write. She droned on like a slow news day.

....

I thought back to my own summer trip and the excitement when my mother first hinted at a *surprise* hidden in our impending journey. She never could keep a secret, especially one like this. Uncle Gus had told the Old Man that when we arrived at the farm, he had something altogether amazing in store for my brother and me. A *surprise*!

....

"Come on Moose, your Dad's honking the horn. It sounds like a tugboat; he might blow the hood off your two-door Ford. Your Dad likes to keep a schedule," Mickey said and then nudged me along. It was near the end of August, the prairie was dry and the grass beneath my feet sounded like I was stepping on corn flakes as I carried my paper Piggly Wiggly grocery bag packed with all I'd need for the week long vacation. Mickey and I were the last to crawl into the black '49 Ford. The Old Man had spent hours that morning waxing the old sedan and it shined like a coffin as he backed onto 4th Street and pointed her east. My brother, Mike, and I shared the soft cushioned back seat with Mickey and of course, our dog Duchess, a black long-haired mongrel we'd rescued from the pound a year ago. Up front, in first class, the Old Man gripped a steering wheel more suitable for a paddle wheeler in his right hand and a Chesterfield, half-smoked in his left hand. My mother, the navigator, lunch packer, and safety monitor settled into the right side with a cup of coffee clutched tightly with both hands, ready to scream out warnings.

"Watch," Mickey whispered. He pushed his open hand through the small window. It caught the air and began dancing like a mad kite. "What are you doing?" I asked hoping that one day he would actually give me a peek into the mystical mystery that was his mind.

"Flying. It's how airplanes fly."

I poked my hand beside his. The air caught and lifted it magically. "Why does it do that?" I didn't get an answer because the Ford pulled to a stop beside the gas pump in Bernie's Standard and my hand crashed to the side of the door. Must be how airplanes became news stories, I concluded.

"Fill her up," the Old Man ordered when Toady, Bernie's pimpled faced young attendant, rushed to our side, orange rag in hand, "...and forget the oil and tires, I already checked her."

The starting line of every trip was the black air hose which announced the departure of each vehicle from the gas pumps at Bernie's. The old Ford never saw a full tank of gas unless we were embarking on a long trip, which was once a year, but for the occasional funeral requiring our attendance. Otherwise it was "put a dollar's worth in." Not today, it was "Fill her up," we're leaving town. We left Mandan only to travel back to my father's home, a place we just called 'the farm.' In our family, it was recognized that 'the farm' meant the place where my grandparents had raised a family of ten and where three brothers and a sister still sweated over the soil and under the cows to scratch out a living and keep America fed. So once a year, at harvest time, our family, like a flock of migrating geese, headed back to where it all began once it had come to an end in Norway.

This trip promised to be different, however. While Mike buried his nose in James Joyce's *Ulysses*, Mickey and I huddled next to the dog and speculated on the surprise that waited a hundred miles away. "Maybe Uncle Gus will give you the farm while you're still young and he can teach you. He's always said it was too much work and he wanted to go back to Norway."

"No, I don't think it will be the farm. Uncle Gus's last gift was a pair of black socks. That'd be a big jump to an entire farm."

Mickey scratched his head with hair closely shaved like a Buddhist monk, "Maybe an ant farm like the one that's for sale at Woolworth's."

"I hope not!"

Mack the Knife played loudly on the scratchy AM radio, my mother hummed and the dog kept time with her tail.

"A jack knife. He has a couple of them. A jack knife can be one of the most useful tools on the planet especially on the farm or if you're lost in the woods and have to kill a bear or have to go off to war and open a can of beans. You told him once you'd like one…"

Our speculation was cut short when the Old Man veered the sedan into the first stop, Crystal Springs. As best I can recall Crystal Springs had two draws, fresh water and a place to get rid of the same. Mike, Mickey, and I bailed from the car and sprinted to the fresh water. The dog raced beside us and nipped at our heels. She fancied herself a herding dog the likes of Lassie and at least in her dreams kept a thousand sheep trotting back to the home place after being scattered by a pack of wolves. Back home, she took special delight in herding the three-wheeled motorcycle driven by the Mandan Police. It wasn't as though they needed any particular place to be herded to since they well knew the trail to the free hamburgers and coffee at Ohm's Café.

The dog and us boys drank our fill of cool water from the hand pump spout, then found a bush to pee behind, and initiated a game of retrieve with Duchess. She had her own version of that game. We would throw the stick and she would dash like a greyhound after the stuffed rabbit to the stick but then added a new twist, my brother and I would have to chase her to get the stick back. The game was cut short when Mom called us back to the car. We piled in, Duchess still clutching the stick.

If the Ford didn't overheat, blow a tire, or lose a belt, we'd be at our next stop by noon. In some ways, it was the favorite stop, although not always in the same place. Mom would sing out, "Oh, Dad, there's a pretty place with shade. Let's stop there." She had a keen eye for selecting the perfect place to give the Old Man some relief from the sun beating down on the left arm he always stuck out his window and from the other drivers who irritated him as much as the sunburn would that night. Shade was one criteria, although cooling off the driver was my mother's main aim. When the Old Man pulled the Ford off the two lane, we needed a smooth spot with shade so Mom could lay the plaid blanket out on the grass. And a grove of trees where a person could respectfully disappear to fulfill any personal needs, sometimes with the roll of TP in hand. So as we drove north out of Crystal Springs, Mom began to assess each potential site.

Distracted by her duty, Mom failed to keep an eye on the activities in the back seat. Duchess had brought the stick into the car and still clenched it tightly in her jaws, waiting for the next stop when we could chase her again. It wasn't long when the heat got the best of her, and she dropped the stick on the seat to get a better grip on panting. As quick as a rat terrier on a ball, Mike grabbed the stick, without looking up from the library book and tossed it out the window.

Duchess, having already been rescued from death row, challenged her fate once more. Over my lap, and out the window, her tail slapped me in the face as she flew past. Mickey made a grab for her and missed but for a few strands of hair from her silky tail. "OOoops," he whispered in the understatement of my childhood. My mouth hung open. Never had I been witness to such a stunning sudden spectacle. And neither had my mother and she commenced to scream like Cathy P. during the matinee showing of *13 Ghosts*.

My brother, Mickey, and I revolved as one and peered over the rear window deck just in time to see the old black dog land in the ditch and spin head over paws a couple of times. A dog leaping from a 1949 Ford moving at fifty miles per hour will create a response in anyone with a heartbeat. The Old Man who had the reaction time of a feather-weight boxer, dynamited the brakes and unleashed a string of profanities that may have had to do with sex or God or both, although it was something I'd need a lifetime to sort out. We rocketed from the rear deck into the back of the front seats, setting off screams from the right side of the car and another explosion of curses from the driver's seat as the Old Man failed in his struggle to keep the

Ford on the road. The ditch was rough and we all clearly heard the boulder strike the car's underside just before the Ford came sliding to a halt. Then there was silence. I suppose we were all thinking the same thing, no one wanted to say it. The dog would be dead, and although she was no Lassie, we still loved her and she still was family.

The Old Man renamed that dog with a half-dozen four letter words when she stuck her face through his window. "Oh, my lord, Dad, she's alive." It's much easier to quote my mother when reciting such events as her verbiage tended to follow along Biblical lines. Praise the Lord, Sweet Jesus, and the like typically preceded her declarations. Mike was out the door as fast as the black dog had flown through the window and picked her up. Cradled in his arms she whined what seemed like an apology. Mike carried her carefully back into the car where she lay between us. My mother leaned over the front seat, did some preliminary probing and poking then concluded we'd just witnessed a miracle on par with Lazarus jumping out of the crypt. As if it was good luck, Duchess still held the stick tightly in her jaws and didn't let go until we'd arrived at the farm and she had to abandon the stick to terrorize the chickens.

The Ford lurched out of the ditch striking two or three more boulders inspiring my mother to launch a hasty prayer for the old Ford. The engine also seemed a bit upset by the rough trip back to the highway and began to growl rather than purr as the Old Man preferred. Our family roadster was beginning to sound more like the hotrods driven down Main Street by the town hoodlums every Saturday night. I liked it, however it was a distinction my mother failed to appreciate, "Good gravy, Dad, what's that noise?"

"Ah, yeah, that's nothing. Damn rotten nuisance of a dog anyway. We must have knocked the muffler loose. I'll fix it when we stop for lunch."

As we resumed our course toward the perfect lunch stop, I was already writing on my mind's scratch pad, the introduction to the inevitable reflection on "What I Did During My Summer Vacation." Now a dog leaping from the Ford flying down the highway would be a pretty good opening anecdote and it would still be within the confines of honesty if I elaborated upon our side trip into the ditch as a 360 rollover survived by all. A few more highlights and embellishments of that quality, not to mention the certain surprise that waited, I wouldn't have to take a back seat to Cathy P.'s trip to Disneyland which on the last day of school she'd proudly announced her family would take in July.

"There under the cottonwood trees." My mother's proclamation jolted me back from one of my occasional trips into orbit with Mickey as my navigator. A sharp turn on two wheels that would make a rum runner proud, brought us into a stand of cottonwood trees. The dog with her stick was the first out followed by my brother, my friend, and me, all anxious to spell our initials in the dry soil with the water from the Crystal Springs. Just like Stephen at Sandymount Strand my brother commented. Mickey and I were left to wonder if this was a friend or some character in Mike's book.

The artistic flourishes I endeavored to add to my work never won praise from my parents, but I was always amazed that art could be produced with such a basic tool and a little imagination. Once, after consuming a king-size Coke on my own, I had enough in the way of resources to leave an A+ next to my handiwork. It was the only A+ I'd ever received. Mickey emptied enough of Crystal Springs to do a portrait of my brother, except for his left ear before he ran out. Nonetheless, a remarkable resemblance, flat top haircut and all.

By the time we'd chased the dog a few laps around the cottonwoods, my mother had laid out summer sausage sandwiches, cheese, and pickles. They enjoyed their black coffee from a thermos and the Old Man finished the lunch with a Chesterfield, unfiltered, and a compliment on the fine cuisine.

I tried to get Mike involved in the speculation of what gift Uncle Gus had waiting for us. "You'll find out when we get there," was all he muttered and returned to reading.

"It's another dog," Mickey suggested in a manner that sealed it as fact. "...you could use another dog to be on watch when Duchess sleeps and it would be somebody she could talk to. It must get lonely for her."

"No, my father had promised that 'Never again' would there be another dog or cat."

"A pig. A big fat spotted pig. You could put a saddle on her and ride it in the 4th of July Parade."

"I hope not. I can still remember the last pig my father brought home. He cut it up in the garage and made head cheese from the eyes and the brain."

"A monkey? Think how easy it would be to get apples if you could send your monkey up the tree. They're smart, too. It was a monkey that was driving the Russian's space ship. I bet a monkey could at least ride a bike and you could sell tickets to watch him in your garage. "

"Does Uncle Gus look like the kind of guy who'd give monkeys away?"

"Larry, come here and hold the flashlight," the Old Man said with another Chesterfield dangling from his lips and a pair of pliers and some baling wire clutched in his hand.

As promised, he crawled under the chassis and with a flashlight with the illuminating power of yesterday's candle, I settled on the ground next to him.

He switched to the silver Zippo lighter eliciting a warning from Mom about blowing us all up. "Who knows Dad, that gas tank might have a leak." She lay on her stomach and handed him tools and advice. He muttered not a word but groaned a lot as though someone was twisting his arm. The three of us and the dog lay next to our mother waiting for the next crisis. Experience had taught us that some calamity was likely and a guy didn't want to miss that. The expectation was great enough to even draw my brother's attention.

We were disappointed. The Old Man wired the muffler to the tailpipe and hung the exhaust pipe back onto the chassis, all without bloodshed. Before long we headed towards the farm in a sedan that no longer sounded like a dragster running on three cylinders. Every mile closer to what I had guessed wouldn't be a toy or a .22 rifle. Uncle Gus was too practical for the former and Mom would have vetoed the later.

I smelled them before I saw the cows of mismatched colors and patterns that stood chewing their cuds and staring at our arrival. I imagined a couple made some comment like 'Oh, no, that dog is back and it brought those boys.' Mickey spied them first, two ponies, a buckskin and a paint were grazing in the midst of the cows. "It's horses!"

"It's a horse!" I repeated.

"Those belong to the neighbor's kids," Mike said with an air of certainty that blasted my dream. I never understood how he could participate in life with his nose so deeply planted in a book without pictures. It was as if he lived in two realities and preferred the one with pages to the one with people.

We bounced past the freshly painted red barn and into a yard surrounded by pig pens, chicken coups, shops, and granaries, our own Adventure Land for the entire week. The back door was opened and our feet on the ground before the Ford rolled to a stop.

....

"And then there was *Mr. Toad's Wild Ride,* which was my favorite..."
Cathy P. continued her presentation before the class. When Miss Martin
had asked for volunteers to talk about the summer, Cathy P.'s hand flew up
faster than a flushed pheasant and sent my attention flying out the classroom window. I think Miss Martin had planned to have each student make
a presentation this day. If we all took this long, it'd be Christmas by the time
we finished. "Mr. Toad led the way on a wild ride..."

....

A wild ride, indeed, that's what we'd gone on that sunny summer afternoon. It began with our aunt, Mabel, calling us down from swinging across
the hay loft on thick knotted ropes. With the grace of spider monkeys, we'd
seized the long vines and swung back and forth across the loft, finally sur-
rendering our grip and falling heavily into the fresh stacked aromatic hay.
Overhead, pigeons and barn swallows swooped down at us, challenging our
right to be there. Mike, Mickey, and I had been performing death defying
circus stunts when Aunt Mabel poked her wrinkled and kind face into the
barn and pleaded for us to join her in the kitchen. One last triple flip with
a soft landing in the hay near the pitchfork and we scurried up to the big
white house with visions of cake and milk waiting for the three of us. There
was cake, chocolate, and sandwiches, deviled ham, and glass jugs of milk
and coffee. It was all destined for the field where the men were harvesting
golden wheat. We'd get our share out there sitting next to the combines and
trucks, like real men.

While we waited in the kitchen, I pestered my mother about the surprise.
She assured me that Uncle Gus promised he'd deliver after the field work
was done and the evening meal eaten.

It was less than a mile to the waiting men, and wouldn't have been much
of a hike, but Mike imagined another mode of transportation. "Let's harness Toad, the old work horse, up to the cart and drive out." Maybe it was
something out of the book he was reading at the time, but outside the supervision of any adult, it seemed an excellent idea. Within minutes Mickey and
I had the mare with the bulging stomach and sagging back secured by a
worn leather harness to a twin seat homemade cart that squeaked with
every revolution of the two rusty metal wheels. To our admiring eyes, Cin-
derella's carriage was no more beautiful and worthy. Mike brought forth
three milk pails stuffed with lunch and with baling wire, tied them to the

back of the cart. I locked Duchess in the barn and the three of us piled in. With the crack of a whip deftly managed by my greenhorn brother, the dun horse who Mike called Throwaway after a horse he'd just read about in Ulysses, strained in the harness. Mickey cried , "Whoaa," before we even began and then we set off down the dusty trail. The decision about who would drive was resolved with a compromise that found both Mike and me each holding a rein. A strategic decision we'd come to regret.

We rounded the first corner, around the grove of chokecherry trees and onto the rutted gravel road. The ripe summer air was filled with scents of diesel fuel mixed with the earthy odor of chopped straw and equine gas as the wind filtered through the mare's tail and into our faces. Mickey, not one to be content with the pace of a trot, gave a light tap on her rear. That in itself wouldn't have produced the catastrophe we were charging towards. No, the fuse that ignited Toad's Wild Ride was lit by the little black dog. Angered by her abandonment, she sensed our disappearance, about the time we cleared Preacher's Hill. A blind newt could have followed the squeaky wheels and the dog had us in her sights by the time we'd reached the valley. Now it was revenge. The dog set upon the horse's hooves like a jackal on a limping wildebeest. Maybe it was also inspired by what he was reading or maybe he was paying more attention to the Old Man than I thought. Mike unleashed a string of curses that would have stunned our father and killed our mother but didn't faze Duchess as she aimed her muzzle low at our helpless horse.

Off the road and into the ditch we flew. Deviled ham sandwiches and jars of milk and coffee were instantly suspended in mid-air then crashed to the ground. Only the barbed wire fence kept Toad from galloping into the river. She galloped down the ditch at a Kentucky Derby winning pace. Mike, who had strained hard on his rein had her thinking about slowing, then when the wheel on his side hit a large rock, he followed the chocolate cake into the air and into the long prairie grass. I struggled with the other rein although only succeeded in turning her back onto the road. Onto the gravel and down the road, the squeaking wheels sounding like a braking locomotive spurred the equine's panic. "Whoooa..." yelled Mickey with such glee the horse could not have possibly misunderstood to be a command. Down the winding road we raced to the bridge where the five spoke wheel finally took flight to the left. My butt puckered so fast, I sucked my underwear out of sight. To the right, the little cart caught some air and Mickey and I flipped into the river.

It was late evening before the men found Toad grazing in a neighboring pasture as if nothing had happened. And Duchess, well, we thought it best to keep her part in the fiasco to ourselves. Her standing in the family was less stable than an NFL coach's tenure in a losing season. The Old Man had issued a standing threat to the little dog, 'Just one more time, and you're going back to the pound.' And our mother, well she spent the afternoon tending to a list of contusions, abrasions, and concussions that would have kept an emergency room in a STAT mode for the day. Forget Cathy P. and Disneyland...that was Toad's Wild Ride.

We were in bed and snoring by the time the men returned from the field most likely complaining about one mechanical breakdown after another. Uncle Gus's secret would have to wait a day.

....

Cathy P. wasn't finished when my attention returned to the front of the class. "And I saw Jiminy Cricket, Donald Duck, the Three Little Pigs..."

....

Pigs! I swore I'd never ever touch a pig again. I even swore off bacon and ham. Nothing ever to do with pigs again. After the last encounter with the sows and their offspring – all tomorrow's pronto pups – I'd joined the millions of Muslims and Jews in their eschewing of the swine. It wasn't always that way, prior to that fateful summer vacation I even counted myself amongst the admirers of the Sus scrofa domesticus.

It was Mickey's idea. At the time, it seemed inspired, although he'd probably been waiting for a chance to introduce the idea since he first pictured the thought the day before. Ride a pig. Not the big sows with a dozen sucklings, each following a swollen teat, or the big boar himself. That would be suicidal. Off in their own pen were the yearling barrows, castrated males. The Old Man had to explain that condition to us. We'd asked Mom what a barrow was, and she referred us to our father for such a delicate articulation on the principles of animal husbandry. Stunned by the brutality inflicted upon these witless creatures, I went to sleep that night clutching my own privates for fear that such a fate might await me as my brother had suggested in a whispered promise during supper.

Back to Mickey's idea to ride a pig. We'd already mastered calf-riding, or stated more accurately, calf-sitting. They had been difficult to mount and even tougher to hang on to, although once we set the time limit to two seconds, we were able to proclaim the animal tamed more often than not. Now the pigs, they seemed so ponderously slow and were much lower to the ground. And none of us had ever seen a bucking pig. Roll in the mud, root in the slop, snore in the sun, but never had one done anything to suggest they'd been paying attention to violent acrobatics of the resident bull.

The men had gone to finish the harvest and the women busied themselves in the kitchen. We'd collected the eggs from a couple of dozen pecking and cackling hens and brought the pail to the big house. We were free until mid-morning lunch when we'd walk, not drive a horse carriage, to the wheat field with lunch pails. Boys free on the farm are among the most unfettered creatures on earth. We'd need two ropes, one to lasso the lucky swine and another to use as a riding harness. We picked the shortest ropes available at the calves' corral. Lightweight cotton ropes, filthy and tattered, were carried over our shoulders to the barrows' quarters. The pink even-toed ungulates squinted in the sun at our arrival. It was clear they sensed our evil intent and huddled in a corner away from us. There was safety in numbers and security in the mud puddle. They fidgeted and swayed sizing us up. We did likewise. Finally, Mike settled on a porker that wore the look of a dullard. The three of us slipped under the aged wooden fence and onto the wet soil. Mike flung the coiled rope at the stunned pig, but with a feint that would flabbergast a linebacker the animal dodged away. The others followed, except a spotted oinker who seemed puzzled by the entire affair. He stood his ground even as Mike slipped the noose around his neck. Not a nudge, not a budge or even a snort. We wrapped the second rope around his ample midsection and he seemed pleased with the attention, even turning a bit to allow Mike to tighten the knot.

Before we had crawled under the fence, we'd the foresight to discuss who would take the first ride. Several methods of selection were discussed before we'd settled on rock, paper, scissors. I'd never been particularly successful at that game. I'd always suspected my brother exercised a style that included holding back just a nano-second longer than the other contestants. Not so delayed as to draw a foul still long enough to ensure victory. This day was no exception and I accepted the challenge to take the first ride.

The cooperative little pig stayed still while I climbed the wooden fence to his right. He wore a hint of a grin or maybe it was a smirk. He stayed still as I eased my cowboy boot sans spurs over his left shank. He even seemed to relax as I settled my seat onto the baby back ribs. He shook a little and his ears flattened, but he didn't stir. This wasn't my first rodeo, I'd seen the bronc riders rake their heels into the hide and hair. I clutched the rope, swung one arm over my head, shouted, "Yippee," and dug my heels hard into the hams.

Although it may not be widely known in the city, it turns out pigs can buck and spin and turn on a dime with a nickel for change. I would have gladly let go and take my lumps, but my fist was locked in the knot my brother, the Boy Scout, had so carefully tied on the patient pig. I yelled for rescue but Mike and Mickey had already bailed onto neutral ground. By the fourth or fifth buck and spin, I settled in to the ride. I had nowhere to go unless I left my arm behind so I clenched my thighs on the porker tighter than a murky water crocodile's jaw clenched on a fat warthog's tail. I got into rhythm with the pig. At least until he altered his strategy. I knew instinctively, I was not dealing with an average mud rolling slop chewing pig. This guy was clever and I should have spotted that smirk and figured that out earlier.

He stopped. Stopped twisting, stopped bucking, stopped squirming, and even stopped squealing. He just stood in the middle of the pen. Then he glanced back over his left shoulder, gave a primeval grunt and fell sideways into the filthiest poop filled mud puddle within 100 acres. I followed him down with a thud. He lay there for the briefest time then rolled and I rolled with him. With the grace of a circus elephant standing with one leg on a four foot orb, he balanced on his spine, all four legs kicking skyward. I choked and sputtered. I spit and cursed. I squirmed and with Herculean effort pulled my hand free of the knot. The pig seemed to sense this and mercifully, rolled to his right, leaving me in the puddle. He got to his knees and then to his hoofs. He shook, turned his tail towards me and loosed a final ball of excrement at my feet.

Pigs, nope, I want nothing to do with them. Don't want to ride them, eat them, and especially don't want to hear any of Cathy P.'s fanciful tales about The Three Little Pigs.

....

Miss Martin had left the classroom to take Lefty Brunel to the nurse. Lefty had chucked up his wieners in the coatroom as he made a dash to the bathroom. I'm not certain it wasn't a commentary on Cathy P.'s Disneyland travelogue which was, with the teacher absent, free to continue ad nauseum. "...so my father took Martin, that's my brother, to the Frontierland Shootin' Arcade and they shot rifles and..."

....

Shootin'. During our summer vacation to the farm, we shot more rounds than a posse in a Western movie. BB guns were always within reach in case some tempting target appeared. Uncle Kermit, dressed in his American Legion Honor Guard uniform topped off with a gleaming silver helmet stood on the wooden steps looking like General Patton himself. "Boys, I want you to get them sons-a-bitches out of the north pasture." He gave us our orders and then marched off to bury a fallen comrade at the Viking Lutheran Church. Sometimes the simplest battle orders are the best and this one gave us great latitude to go after the 13 striped ground squirrel, or gopher as it was commonly known. Not that we had any personal grudge against the buck toothed rodent, but Uncle Kermit had given us direct orders. The little rats were taking over the pasture leaving more holes than a putting green. As Uncle Kermit explained earlier when he put out the hit, the badgers and foxes dig in the gopher holes making them bigger and next thing you know the cows fall into the larger holes and break their legs. "Farming's a business, boys, and those rodents are costing me money."

I believe he applied Christian principles to animals, but he didn't see the need to turn every point into a sermon. We pulled our ball caps down to our ears in the face of a wind that bent the pines tops to the south. That would make our mission difficult. We'd have to allow for windage. The gravel crunched under our black high topped Keds as Mike explained his strategy for the attack. We'd crawl under the barbed wire fence where the plum trees ended and then using the cover of Preacher's Hill, dart to the top. From that vantage we'd have the wind to our back and the high ground. Ever since watching *Pork Chop Hill*, we knew the advantage of taking the high ground.

The plan was executed flawlessly. We arrived at the summit and peered over the top. Sure enough, as Mike had explained, the wind to our backs and the sun over our shoulders, blinding the enemy as they scanned the horizon for coyotes, badgers, and boys. A perfect place of ambush. Dozens of the gophers stood high on their mounds and whistled in the wind. We pumped the guns and opened fire. One polished orb after another left the barrel, and flew towards the vulnerable rodents. One after another fell mercifully short. Out of range and not by a little. We slid back down the hill. Mickey rolled he eyes skyward and put his hands together, palm to palm. I think he was pleased with the predicament.

A new plan was formulated. We'd jog along the fence to the corner by the rock pile then crawl up the smaller hill which would put us in easy range and still control the high ground. With *Blitzkrieg* speed we dashed to the rocks then down the fence line to the hill covered with sage brush. We scratched our way to the top, sweating and breathing hard, yet stealthy, making hardly a sound. The fresh breeze, filled with the odor of cow flop, now in our faces and the sun steadfast in our eyes, we looked over the crest. There they were, only a dozen yards away. They'd been joined by a friend, a black ally with a double white stripe down its back and its tail held high, up wind. As Field Marshall Helmut Graf von Moltke wrote of all great battles, "No campaign plan survives first contact with the enemy."

Aunt Mabel made us undress behind the outhouse and then scrub with lye soap using buckets of water from the stock tanks. We ate outside that night and slept in the barn loft, something we'd been itching to do anyway. Our only companions were the cats who spent the night chasing mice. Banishment to the barn meant one more day before Uncle Gus's big surprise would be forthcoming.

The rooster woke us up the next morning, that and the sounds of milk pails clanging below the loft. I nudged Mickey and then we raced down the rough wooden steps to the milking parlor. Uncle Gus stood separating the cream from the fresh milk. His appearance never varied. Each day he'd don his blue denim work shirt and striped cotton overalls, and a railroader's engineer cap pulled down over his short sandy hair. And every day he wore the same gentle smile. He ran his large calloused hand through my hair and uttered a 'Good Morning' with a thick Norwegian accent. "We'll finish early tonight because it's going to rain. I'll give you and Mike your surprise."

Evening couldn't come fast enough as we helped around the farm doing chores, mostly helping the women, until they left for a Ladies Circle Meeting up at the church. Mickey and I sat on the cellar door with Duchess and Lucky, the 150 pound farm dog who'd eaten his way past productivity. Thunder clouds rose to the West. Uncle Gus was right, rain was coming. Mike had walked out to the field to the east to bring a light lunch. The men would be quitting before dinner.

My brother came running around the corner of the old white house. Sweat dripped from his forehead. Trying to catch his breath, he gasped, "Get Mom... Gus has been hurt. He's caught in the combine. Dad said Mom should bring our car out to the field to give him first aid and drive him to the hospital."

"Mom took the women up to the church. They're all gone. Why didn't Dad come to get the car?"

"Gus is bleeding real bad and Dad's trying to stop it. He can't leave. Uncle Gus needs to get to the hospital or he'll bleed to death." It was as if one of the most dramatic moments in his cherished novel was playing out before him.

Without explanation, Mike turned and ran. Mickey and I followed although I was uncertain where we were going. The church was three miles away and running back to the field where Uncle Gus lay seemed counterproductive even to my young mind unaccustomed to life and death matters. Mike sprinted to the open shed door where the dilapidated pickup was spending its last days.

"You can't drive!" I shouted.

Pessimism has no place in a crisis. Mike jumped into the driver's seat. Mickey and I followed. A '36 International Harvester pickup would be the last lesson in the advanced drivers' course. Starting it required at least three feet and an extra hand. On the floor, you had to pump the gas pedal, depress the brake, push in the clutch, and depress the floor starter button, pretty much simultaneously. On the dash, the manual choke needed tending, and the steering wheel manned, while shifting the stick to change gears. With what would seem miraculous guidance, we managed with teamwork as artful as the Explorer astronauts to drive the truck to the field where Gus lay on the ground next to the combine. My father carried our wheezing Uncle Gus to the truck box, laid him down gently, and crawled in next to him to maintain the pressure on the hemorrhaging artery. My father ordered us back into the cab where we were to 'drive like hell.' I didn't need to add that it was the only way my brother knew how to drive.

....

"You boys take a turn," Uncle Kermit ordered and handed each of us a shovel. The grave was only four feet deep when the three of us jumped in.

Above us, the men spoke of how proud Gus would be watching, from heaven, his favorite nephews were pitching in. They talked about how my father couldn't have done anything more to prevent Gus from bleeding to death and that the 'boys' had acted like men driving that old truck to town to save their uncle. A bottle of Everclear sweetened with burnt brown sugar was passed as the men conversed and smoked.

We weren't experienced grave diggers and as such, without much supervision, we dug too far to the left. It wasn't that Uncle Gus would mind being a little closer to his brother, Oscar, but Oscar, or his remains, paid an unexpected visit to our excavation. Without a vault, Oscar's pine box had rotted and when Mike's shovel pierced the bottom, it released an odor that sent us flying out of the grave. Uncle Kermit caught up with us in the gravel parking lot and explained that "These things happen. Why I remember..." and an hour later the problem was solved with thick rough planks and we were back digging.

We stayed an extra week on the farm to get the grain out of the fields and in the bins. Mike learned to drive the pickup and pulled a grain trailer between the bins and the field. Mickey and I learned to drive the little Ford tractor and pulled wagons and ran errands. By the end of the 'vacation' we were tanned and exhausted, and life had changed for us. Not just because Uncle Gus was gone, but we had changed.

．．．．．．．．．．．．．．．．．

"....and I met Mickey Mouse and Minnie Mouse and Woody Woodpecker..." Cathy P. had enough material to fill the school year and Miss Martin still hadn't returned. Mr. Barnyard, the janitor, had arrived with a bucket and a mop to clean up after Lefty. Thankfully, he opened the windows and let some fresh air blow over the class. Like Cathy P.'s rendition, it was getting stale, if not revolting in the room. "...and then there was Goofy..."

．．．．．．．．．．．．．．．．．

Uncle Lawrence looked like Goofy. Or maybe Goofy looked more like Uncle Lawrence. Tall, big droopy ears, and friendly eyes. Although in his seventies, he still walked like a clumsy adolescent who hadn't grown into his height and size 13 shoes. And he was as gregarious and accepting as the cartoon character. That's where the similarities end, as Uncle Lawrence was as wise a man who ever lived. He never married still he often said a man with a big wife and a big barn is a lucky man, indeed. In fact, Uncle Lawrence spoke in parables and folksy sayings. It was he who told me Uncle Kermit went to the funeral because his friend, "bought the farm." And when Duchess lurked around the chicken coop, it was Uncle Lawrence who told me about "letting the fox in the chicken coop." And then there was "shutting the barn door after the horses had run out." I'd just learned that barns have two doors. Duchess had discovered that when we'd left her in the barn to deliver the lunch.

When I was older, Uncle Lawrence gave me one last pearl of wisdom to hold on to. He said, "A happy man marries the girl he loves; a happier man loves the girl he marries."

....

Cathy P. became Cathy B. when we exchanged wedding vows. My wise Uncle Lawrence, who never failed me with his advice, was right and I'm a happier man for it. Disneyland hasn't been in our travel plans. However the annual summer vacation to the farm has become our family tradition. We still stop at Crystal Springs. We plant flowers on Uncle Gus's grave. My mother, gone to a place where every day is a picnic under the cottonwoods, would be proud to know Cathy B. picks the same places of peace, serenity and togetherness as she had decades earlier.

During one lazy trip to the farm, I shared this story with Cathy. I told her about the anticipation of the big surprise and how it didn't seem so important after Uncle Gus 'bought the farm.' Mike and I were so busy filling Uncle Gus's boots that the subject wasn't even discussed until we were nearly home. It was the Old Man who brought it up. "You boys know what Uncle Gus's surprise was?"

I'd lost interest in even guessing.

"He told me that it was time to treat you like men and he was going to teach you to drive so that you could help with the harvest. And he made you each one of these." My mother handed us a wooden shingle decorated with engraving done with a hot scrolling iron. In the day, it was art although unless produced by an Italian fashion photographer in his quaint upstate New York studio, it would no longer be considered as such. Mine was burned with images of running horses. I read the inscription out loud,

"When I was a child, I spoke and thought and reasoned as a child. But when I grew up, I put away childish things."

The surprise? He'd given us the gift of manhood. It couldn't have been more wonderful and unexpectedly, Uncle Gus delivered it from his grave.

L.D. Bergsgaard retired as a Special Agent after nearly thirty years in law enforcement and currently resides in Minnesota and Arizona with his wife of forty years, Donna. They share their home with a one eyed Pug named the same, Gunner, the world's best dog, and a buckskin mare named Ruby all abandoned by their lovely daughters, Kate and Anne.

L.D. Bergsgaard is the author of the Doc Martini series, *Next Year in Jerusalem*, *While Others Sleep*, and *Rumors*.

CPSIA information can be obtained
at www.ICGtesting.com
Printed in the USA
FSOW02n1136041214
3702FS

9 781457 510342